Lovers & Friends

The R&B Series Book 3

Lovers & Friends

The R&B Series Book 3

By Olivia Linden

"*I love you without knowing how, or when, or from where. I love you simply, without problems or pride.*" – Pablo Neruda

Thank you to Miss W. You rode the wheels off with me on this one. I appreciate you!

PLAYLIST

Enjoy this playlist inspired by Joey & Shane's story.

Main Playlist.

Shane's Oldies

MAILING LIST

Join my newsletter for updates, giveaways, and upcoming projects

The beginning...

August 2003 / Freshman Year

"Ladies! Welcome to FAMU and to the most important facet of this school's athletic department."

Joey chuckled to herself as the coach of the cheer squad continued her speech. Nervous was an understatement. Her entire being was teeming with excitement laced with a tinge of anxiety. Not only had she been accepted to the FAMU Cheer squad, but she was also one of the top candidates and had been invited to practice over the summer before the semester started. She couldn't wait to meet the other girls and join the crew.

Her nerves were shot because of everything she had to endure to be there.

The boys' basketball team was warming up for their practice session across the gym as the girls were winding down from their first practice. Joey, a natural flirt, was checking out all the players when she locked eyes with the tallest guy on the team. His frame was slim, but wide. His tawny complexion was a near match to hers, and his curly faux-hawk added another dimension to his presence. He shot her a sly smile, catching her watching him, then glanced away when one of the other guys called for his attention. She was captivated by how comfortable he was handling a ball as he bounced and twirled it effortlessly.

"Girl! You did so good today," Kiko, the designated team captain, said with a playful smile.

"Thanks," Joey smiled back. "I was just trying to keep up with you."

"No, you and Nicole got it. I'm gonna need you to help the other girls with the steps when we break into smaller groups. Is that cool with you?"

"Oh, sure," Joey gushed, thrilled to be recognized by the best girl on the squad.

"Great. If you can stay a little later, we can work with a couple of the girls struggling with the steps. We want to be A1 for the season opener in a few weeks. Plus, we're the only freshmen on the squad. We gotta be on point."

Joey nodded in agreement. She hadn't expected to make first string after only two tryouts. That's why she was so hyped. Even though she knew her skills were top-notch and had been in dance competitions since she was a young girl living in New Orleans with her grandmother. Dancing was not only her passion, but it was in her blood as both her mother and grandmother were blessed with the talent.

Her mother was a dancer who had traveled around the country performing with various bands until she hurt herself and settled in California. Well, that's the story she told. The real story was that her mother had a bad habit of choosing the wrong men and having babies they didn't want. Joey's father was very wealthy but also very married and had no intentions of leaving his wife. She left Joey with her grandmother to continue traveling until she got pregnant again.

That baby she couldn't just drop off.

Refusing to return to Louisiana as a failure, her mother chose to settle down in Oakland as a dance teacher for a local middle school. She'd sent for Joey in the ninth grade, and it didn't take long to deduce that she needed a babysitter more than she had missed her oldest child. Joey hated being away from her grandmother, who wasn't in the best of health, but both women felt that moving with her mother was the right thing to do.

Immediately after graduating from high school, Joey left Oakland for Louisiana to spend part of the summer with her grandmother before heading to college. She enrolled in the communications program at Florida A&M University, which would allow her to focus on becoming a publicist. It was also closer to her grandmother. Her master plan was to be a successful businesswoman and find an even more successful businessman who could and would take care of her—definitely not any entertainers with a legion of groupies.

FAMU was about as far as she could get from her mother without leaving the country.

Joey worked two jobs to save money and pay the extra tuition fees to stay in the dorms the following semester. It would be a struggle, but she was determined to do whatever it took. Returning to Oakland was not an option, and neither was failure. One night after her shift at Dairy Queen, she came home to find an envelope on her pillow. Tired yet curious, she opened it to find an old bank book with a balance of twenty thousand dollars. Her eyes bulged out of her head.

"I know it's not a lot," her grandmother's soft Cajun accent floated across the room from the doorway where she stood with her cane.

"Grann," Joey gasped, still in shock. She didn't know how she was going to make things work, but she had no choice. She was never going to be reliant on anyone to take care of her and planned to bust her ass if she had to.

"It should be a lil cushion for you with your fancy scholarship. You gone have to make it stretch the best you can," the older woman continued.

Joey felt her chest tighten as the only person who had ever really held her down, came through for her once again. She knew her grandmother didn't have a lot, and the fact that she sacrificed to put money aside to help support her made her emotional. Tears welled up in her eyes as her grandmother sat on her twin-sized bed and pulled Joey into a warm embrace.

"Now, don't you be cryin', girl. You know I'ma always take care of my baby."

"Thank you, Grann. I wasn't sure how to pull this off, but I have to do it." Joey sniffed. She tried her best to reign in her emotions, but all that she had been through and the significant change ahead of her was overwhelming.

"I believe in you, child. I see your determination. And even if those two damn fools masquerading as your parents don't have your back, I will. As long as I have breath."

Joey just nodded as she absorbed her grandmother's words.

"And you know I don't usually tell you what to do,"

"Ok," Joey encouraged her to continue.

"Keep your focus. Don't let no man sidetrack yuh. My girl is beautiful, and the men will just come a-knockin'. Have your fun, but don't get carried away."

"Yes, ma'am." Joey nodded dutifully.

"But, one day, there will be a man that'll feel like magic. It'll scare you, but that's the one you want to hold on to. The one that makes you feel safe enough to be your true self. You remind me so much of your mama, and she let all ha greatness go to waste chasin' afta dat wrong man."

It had been a bittersweet moment for Joey because as excited as she was to start building the future of her dreams, a small part of her wanted to stay in the comfort of her grandmother's little house in the 4th Ward. Her grandmother's words inspired her to give her all to the dance squad. Not only did she want to secure a spot, but she was looking forward to the experience of being a part of one of the most well-known HBCU athletic squads.

So, she showed up to practice early every day and stayed late to help Kiko work with the few girls who needed extra assistance. Nicole, another freshman on the squad, was also top tier with her moves. The three of them gravitated toward each other and soon formed a bond where they would hang out together after practice. During one of their courtside tutoring sessions, a basketball came rolling and bounced against Joey's leg. Squatting, she scooped the ball up and was about to throw it back across the gym when a tall figure approached her, arms outstretched.

It was the boy who had smiled at her.

"Sorry about that," his velvety-smooth voice floated over her head. Way over her head as he towered a good seven to eight inches over her 5'9" frame. Joey craned her neck upwards, trying not to gawk as his pouty lips spread apart, showcasing his perfect teeth as he flashed her a dazzling smile.

"That's ok," she said, finally finding her voice again. Then, to defuse the tension stirring between them, she added, "Just don't let it happen again."

He chuckled. "My bad. I'll do my best, ma'am."

"Ew, my grandmother is *ma'am*. I'm Joey." She tucked the ball under her arm and offered her hand.

"Shane," he replied, his smile widening as he took her smaller hand in his. When they touched, he looked her up and down, his eyes twinkling with curiosity. Joey felt a blush creeping up her neck as she slowly pulled away. He smelled of fresh laundry and male sweat which was driving her crazy.

"Damn, she thick!" She heard one of his teammates say from behind him, which caused her to blush even harder. Shane' eyes traveled over her again, taking inventory like he'd missed something before. The smile that curved his lips when his eyes rested on her thighs made her tremble inside, but her expression remained a smirk.

"Do you always smile so much, *Shane*?" Her question came just as the other team members urged him to hurry up. Reaching for the ball, he shrugged as he turned away.

"Hey," he called over his shoulder. "Life is good."

Joey wasn't the type to get all silly over a guy, and she wasn't about to start. But Shane was cute in a unique way. Tall, slim, yet muscular, his features were a mixture of bold, masculine lines in his jaw and forehead with high cheekbones and full lips. His deep-set eyes twinkled a mix of green and browns and turned up at the corners with ridiculously long lashes. His curly hair was dyed blonde, but the roots were dark, giving his look a bit of an edge, along with the crown tattoo that wrapped around his neck.

Someone clearing their throat behind her snapped her back to the present.

"You think we can finish workin' on these moves, or you want to work on something else?" Nicole teased.

"Definitely not," Joey denied. "I just don't think I've ever seen someone that tall in real life."

"Yeah, he was tall. And is it me, or was he kinda cute? His eyes are so pretty!" Kiko waggled her brows at Joey.

"Kinda, right? He's lanky as hell. But the curly fro thing is working for him," Nicole chimed in.

"And you know what they say about those tall and skinny boys." Kiko wagged her brows as Joey animatedly rolled her eyes. "Just stay away from Jay. I'm sure he already introduced his fast self."

Joey giggled. "He did."

"You can just tell he's a player," Nicole scowled.

Kiko laughed. "He can't keep them girls off him."

"Ok, ladies. I only have about a half hour before I have to leave for work," Joey said, putting an end to their distraction.

"Oh, *now* you want to get focused," Nicole said as she playfully nudged Joey's shoulder. "Well, I'll walk with you 'cause I'm craving an Oreo Blizzard."

"Ooh, that sounds yummy! I'm in," Kiko said as she motioned for the girls to hit their spots.

That was another reason Joey found herself clicking with those two girls. They didn't make her feel funny for having to work at a fast-food spot to earn some extra cash. What they didn't know was that she needed the job to pay for her off-campus housing, since she couldn't afford housing when she enrolled. The money from her grandmother would help, but not for long, and she'd have to wait until the next semester to get into the dorms. In the meantime, the efficiency unit behind the local Waffle House restaurant would have to do.

It wasn't that Joey was embarrassed for anyone to know her struggles; she just didn't want anyone to feel sorry for her. She was tough, had been through a lot, and was determined to make her own way. Having a wealthy father who refused to help and a mother who was too disconnected to be concerned with her daughter's needs drove her to be able to take care of herself at all times. She refused to allow anyone to disappoint her again.

Chapter 1

"Oh! This view! I think I could live out here forever," Joey raved as their chartered yacht glided over the serene blue waters of Lake Como, Italy. Sipping a glass of champagne, she smiled serenely, turning her face up to the sun. Determined to deepen her summer complexion, she laid on a lounge chair toward the boat's bow.

As far as everyone knew, she was in Italy visiting Nicole and Jay, two of her closest friends from college who also happened to be a couple. Her real reason was to celebrate her best friend Shane's birthday. He was in Europe for a few NBA preseason games and was able to finagle a few days to spend with his friends, but mainly to see Joey.

"It is gorgeous," Nicole agreed. "I just wish I could really enjoy it. I swear, being seasick is worse than having morning sickness."

Nicole, who was four months pregnant, looked stunning in her white bathing suit with

11

her slight baby bump. She was trying but failing to overcome her queasiness.

"My poor baby. You're turning green like Oscar the Grouch. Want to go lie down?" Jay, Nicole's fiancé, pampered her on a good day, but her pregnancy had him on ten. He rubbed her stomach as he handed her a glass of ginger ale. His reference to the grumpy character caused the group to chuckle as Nicole flashed one of her infamous eye rolls before conceding.

"I think I might need to. Seeing the scenery moving is what's killin' me. Sorry, guys."

"Aww," Joey cooed. "Don't worry about it, *Boo*. Just feel better."

"I brought some of those chewy ginger candies for you. I'll get them from my bag," Shane replied.

"Thanks, man," Jay said, giving Shane's fist a pound. He helped Nicole, guiding her gingerly as if she were much further along. Joey smiled, loving how attentive he was toward her. She watched the three disappear below deck, noticing the newest tattoo on Shane's back. It was a heart that matched one she had on her wrist. He'd told her he was going to get it, but she didn't believe him.

When he returned, she couldn't help but check him out. When they first met, he'd been so tall and skinny, but his body definitely caught up to his height over the years. Shane had transformed into a fine-ass specimen of a man with an edgy style. Tattoos and piercings were just a form of expression, like artwork. She salivated just at the sight of him.

Shane reached for a beer from one of their coolers and settled in a deck chair next to where Joey was sunbathing.

"I love how he treats her like a fragile princess," Joey joked.

Shane grinned. "I know, right?"

"Am I more shocked that they're together, or how he's a changed man?"

"I'm not shocked," Shane replied after a long gulp. "He always said that once he found 'the one,' he wouldn't have a problem settling down. We just didn't believe him."

"True," Joey agreed, looking over at him. She had been trying not to stare at him all day, with his golden-tipped coils hanging wild and his skin sporting a nice sun-kissed summer glow. With his shirt off, Shane's heavily inked torso was on full display. Her lips unconsciously puckered when she let her eyes wander to the sizeable bulge in his swim trunks.

"Do you think it's just that easy? To change like that. Going from a player to fiancé of the year?"

Shane thought about it for a moment before responding. Joey handed him a bottle of mango-coconut scented oil to rub on her back and turned onto her stomach. He drizzled a pattern all over her before massaging it in.

"I don't really think it's a change, so to speak. That's who Jay always was. It was just dormant."

Joey laughed.

"I'm serious," Shane insisted. "I think we do a disservice to ourselves by putting people in boxes like that."

"Let's be real, though. Most people who shun monogamy can't just flip a switch. I think it becomes inherent to want the freedom of multiple options."

Shane looked down at her and frowned. "I disagree. Sometimes it depends on the conditions. Some people just know what they want and aren't willing to settle or pretend until they get it."

"Ahh, and now we're talking about *you*," Joey noted.

"It's not just me."

"I guess," she replied.

"You don't think you'd change for the right man?"

Joey gave him the side eye. "What's that supposed to mean?"

"You know what I mean. Being monogamous for the right person."

"Oh, I *know* I can."

"So why are you settling for an open relationship with Dante?"

Joey didn't respond right away because not only was she pondering the question, but the way Shane's hands had begun caressing her back instead of spreading the suntan oil and the way he said *settling* had her feeling *unsettled*. She held his eye contact, a fatal mistake because his smoldering glare struck her.

"I'm not settling." She denied. "This is what works for me right now."

"If you say so," he replied, fingers tracing the tattoo on her upper back. He had the matching heartstring on his.

"So, for Jay, he was waiting for the right conditions, but for me, it's settling?"

She struggled to get the words out because the way he was kneading and stroking her bare skin was distracting at that point. Joey hated that Shane was able to arouse her so simply. Ever since Kiko's wedding, he'd had been coming at her with the idea of elevating their friendship from the vague "friends with sometimes benefits" classification to something more serious. And if she were honest, she'd always considered it, but him being in the NBA with women literally throwing themselves at him day and night gave her pause.

"Yeah, it's settling," he insisted.
"Because?"
"Because you have a better option."

Joey let his words hang between them. His hands were manipulating her lower back, his pinky tracing the seam of her bikini bottom. They maintained eye contact, his morphing from hazel to a deep amber. His eye color fluctuated with his moods, and when he was aroused, it was like he could see straight through her.

"Stop looking at me like that," she sighed.

"Like what?" He smirked.

Joey wasn't the least bit surprised when he leaned over and kissed her, first softly on the lips and then behind her ear, where he lingered while relishing in her unique fragrance.

"I love this scent," he murmured against the smooth flesh of her neck, causing her to shudder.

"Shane, no," she chided weakly, and he groaned.

"Why?"

"Because," she whined without any real reason.

"You know damn well when you handed me that oil that this was gonna go left," he murmured, grabbing a handful of her thigh and squeezing it. "There's no one around, not even another boat. No fans. No cameras."

Shane leaned back a bit, reinitiating eye contact before leaning in for another kiss when her eyes kept flitting to his lips. He snaked his fingers into her wild, honey-blonde-streaked, natural coils and twirled a few strands around his fingers as his tongue explored her mouth. They'd been doing the same song and dance for years, and Shane was ready for more. There wasn't anyone he could see himself wanting the way he wanted Joey.

Joey moaned and leaned into the kiss. Shane always exuded a tenderness she couldn't resist or get enough of. They shared the kind of chemistry she'd never found with anyone else. Sometimes, she felt he wasn't playing fair because he knew her so well that it was second nature for him to please her. He could be sweet and tender or so fiery and passionate that he burned through all her doubts or reservations.

Shane's hand skimmed down her back and underneath her bikini bottom, skirting the seam of her ass cheeks until he encountered what he was looking for. Joey was so wet it was dripping from her. He swirled his fingers at her entrance, loving the squishing sound that was like music to his ears, before thrusting two fingers inside of her and being rewarded with a tortured moan.

Joey's fingers gripped the edge of her chair. From her vantage point, she could see his other hand slip into his swim trunks as he grabbed and stroked his growing length. The sight of it made her even hotter, and she clenched around his fingers. She reached for his thigh, massaging it and exciting him even more with her touch.

"You're so nasty," she murmured when he matched the pace of the hand inside her with the one around his shaft.

"You love it." His voice was strained as his breathing accelerated. The way he hooked his fingers inside her grazed against her sweet spot with every thrust.

"Mmh," Joey moaned. She rocked her hips as her climax began to peak.

"Yes, baby. Come for me," he groaned.

They both panted swiftly, trying to contain their grunts and moans, excited that someone could catch them at any moment. It wouldn't be the first time Jay caught them in the act because they were spontaneous and would act on their desires whenever the mood arose. No matter when or where.

Knowing how to get him there quicker, Joey rose up on her knees and gripped his hips, brushing his hand away so that she could take him into her mouth. She moaned around his length as it grew firmer against her tongue and basked in his rich, masculine scent. Shane clasped the back of her head as he leaned over her to continue to bring her over the edge. When she began to whimper around his dick, he knew she was close. Rotating his hand, he twisted his fingers and massaged her clit with his thumb. Joey's back bucked as she came all over his hand, which triggered him to come down her throat.

"Damn, Juicy," he murmured as he fought to regain his senses. He grabbed the towel on the back of his chair and wiped between her legs.

Jay's off-key singing as he returned upstairs on the other end of the boat put an official end to their tryst. Shane pulled back reluctantly, slumping into his chair as he resituated his dick back into his trunks. He whispered a request before he leaned back.

"Stay with me tonight." Then he pulled down his shades, masking the emotion blazing behind their reflective lenses. One by one, he sucked her essence from his fingers.

Shaking her head with a grin, Joey fixed her bikini and closed her legs, consenting to his request with a slight nod. She discreetly wiped her mouth before their friend rejoined them.

"Have you kids been behaving?"
"Of course," Shane replied with an angelic grin.
"Sure thing," Joey added.
"Right... I believe you." Jay arched his brow knowingly, then grabbed a Peroni from the cooler and sat in the lounge chair beside Shane's. "Your hair looks really nice, Joey."

She blushed feverishly, smoothing down the wild mass that Shane had disrupted. Jay laughed, shaking his head as he moved on from teasing her.

"I feel for Nicky 'cause she is down bad. She's sleeping now, but we'll probably have to cut the boat ride short so she can get right for your birthday dinner."

"Nah, it's all good. I understand if she can't make it. Baby comes first."

"You crazy?" Jay exclaimed. "She'll be there. Just give her a few hours on steady land. Once the sea sickness subsides, she'll be fine."

"I'll come by to help her get ready," Joey offered.

"She'd love that. You know she plays tough, but I know as much as she loves Italy, she's truly missing her girls. All she does is stalk your social media and talk about everything you guys have going on. She was ecstatic when I told her I was considering trying out for the L.A. teams."

"Oh my God! That would be dope if you guys moved out to Cali." Joey was so excited that she turned around and sat up, ignoring Shane, who was ogling her.

"I know Kiko's gonna feel some type of way about that," Shane chuckled.

"I think Dom's considering leaving Miami," Joey divulged. "Their salary cap isn't gonna allow them to pay him the max contract he deserves. And a few West Coast teams have already expressed interest."

"*And,* I think Remy and Chelle are getting tired of flying across the country whenever it's time to make a deal," Shane replied.

"To the gang coming back together!"

They all raised their drinks to Jay's toast. Joey smiled the brightest because her plan was coming together.

∞

That night, the four friends sat down to a five-star Italian meal for Shane's birthday dinner. They dined on polenta crostini with tuna and baked gorgonzola ravioli for appetizers, beef filet with green peppercorn sauce for a main course, and tiramisu for dessert. Nicole was glowing as she sat hand in hand with Jay, who looked like the happiest man on earth. Joey couldn't help but be happy for her friend, especially after everything she had gone through with her ex. Jay was still his usual comical self, but he was especially serious when it came to Nicole.

Although she and Shane were *not* a couple, the intimate atmosphere brought them closer, and he displayed rare bouts of PDA. These were small things, things that you might expect from two people who had been friends for a long time and were very comfortable with each other, but also familiar touches of two people who had an intimate connection.

It was in the way his hand grazed her arm when he reached across her for the butter or how he gently pushed the tendril of hair behind her ears so he could see her face when she was talking. They shared knowing glances with each other with inside jokes. She ate off his plate without thinking twice, and if he minded, he never showed it.

It was the way her hand rested on top of his whenever she laughed at one of his jokes. Being out of the limelight and with close friends caused them both to let their guard down. At one point, he kissed her cheek, puckering his lips for a kiss while she sipped her wine. Nicole and Jay exchanged shocked glances but were not really that surprised.

"So," Nicole drawled as she glanced between the couple sipping her lemon sparkling water. "Is this confirmed? Are you two *finally* gonna admit there's something going on?"

"There's nothing –" Joey began to reply while Shane answered, "Yes."

"Interesting," Nicole said as she glanced at Jay and mouthed *wow*.

"At this point, what the hell's stopping y'all?" Jay, who never usually got involved, genuinely wanted to know why two of his closest friends denied what was so apparent to everyone else.

"We're working on it," Shane affirmed. Joey just smiled and sipped her wine.

"Well, I'm glad y'all are finally coming to your senses. This charade has been going on for long enough. Don't you think?"

Joey just shook her head at Nicole's forwardness. She glanced at Shane, but he just shrugged. There wasn't much that either of them could say because it had been a long time coming.

September 2003, Freshman Year

The first week of classes had been rough on Joey. Adjusting to waking up at the crack of dawn to get to her class on time was a struggle after the summer practice schedule and then working until close. Working nights and living off-campus was kicking her ass. She had a stacked schedule because Communications was her major, but she also minored in Early Childhood Education. Being a teacher was her first career choice until she learned they made little to no money. Her father refused to help her financially unless she participated in activities he approved of, so she vowed never to need him or anyone again.

Thursday was Joey's last day of classes for the week, and English was her first period. Her coaches had warned her that her professor was a stickler regarding lateness. The campus was a quick bus ride or a long walk from her apartment, so she chose the bus. Smelling like outside was not the impression she was trying to make on her first day.

Joey made it to class with time to spare and took her pre-assigned seat, which happened to be in the middle of the classroom. She used the extra time to study her schedule and plot her routes from class to class. Her last class of the day was calculus, and then she had practice. Then, she headed to work for a four-hour shift. Feeling sorry for herself wasn't the norm, but she was trying to figure out a way to simplify her schedule when a commotion at the doorway caught her attention.

The tall guy from the basketball team was entering the classroom and seemed to have an entourage already. He dressed like a baller in a crisp white T-shirt, FAMU basketball shorts, and a clean pair of black Jordan 8s. His hair was styled in a freshly cut faux-hawk with the blonde tips grown out. He walked with a certain swag that showed he knew he had it going on but also had an approachable air about him. Joey could feel her heart rate speed up when his eyes met hers as he searched for his seat. She almost stopped breathing when he stopped right by her, looked her in her eyes, and smiled as he took the seat in front of her.

"No way," Joey mumbled under her breath.

A few girls crowded his desk, talking to him all at once while he settled in. He didn't seem to be paying any of them much mind, but he also wasn't rude about it. She wasn't sure if was he height or his looks, but there was something about him that made you take notice.

"Ok, class. Let's settle down. I'll take roll, and then we can begin with a short introduction of yourself."

The English teacher closed the classroom door and began to call out the student's names alphabetically as he walked the aisles to verify each student.

"Shane Duncan," he said as he stopped by her friend at the desk in front of her.
"Shane Duncan," the tall guy repeated before launching into his introduction. "You may not guess this about me, but it's my goal to play ball in the NBA." There were laughs and giggles from the other students before he continued. "My major is Sports Management, and I'm here on a full scholarship ride. English is my favorite subject, and Mystery and Suspense is my favorite genre to read."
"Very interesting, Mr. Duncan. What's one of your favorite books?"

Joey's brows rose, figuring he'd be stumped and that he was just kissing up to their teacher, and they climbed even higher when he answered the question.

"Well, I've read *The Postman Always Rings Twice* by James M. Cain and really enjoyed it, but *Devil in a Blue Dress* is one of my favorites," Shane replied.

The teacher merely nodded, but it was apparent he was impressed. Joey felt her stomach flip-flop as it was her turn to introduce herself. Even though she had practiced it in her head repeatedly, she drew a blank after paying such rapt attention to Shane's response.

"Jonelle DuVall?" The teacher paused next to her desk and did a double take. "Are you two related?"

Joey cut her eyes at the professor. Yes, they were both tall and light-skinned, but that didn't have to mean they were related.

"*Joey* DuVall, no relation to the NBA hopeful who's probably a whole foot taller than me."

"Ok, Miss DuVall. Go on," the professor said over the laughter of the other students.

"My major is communications, and I'm also minoring in childhood education. I love working with kids, but I also want to be able to participate in our capitalistic society to the best of my capabilities, so I want to be a publicist when I grow up. I was raised by my Creole grandmother, I can make a mean red beans and rice, and I'm on the Cheer squad."

A few people actually clapped when she finished speaking. Surprised, she glanced around, smiling at those who did. When she faced forward, she was stunned by the piercing gaze of Shane's odd yet beautiful eyes. She couldn't tell if they were a dark green, a light brown, or both. He seemed to admire her with an air of curiosity, almost like he didn't expect what came out of her mouth. Well, that made the two of them because she was just as taken by him.

"Nice," he said, looking down at her fidgeting fingers. "Lemme see your schedule."

"Mine?" She asked, even as she handed him the piece of paper with the folded edges. He turned around, taking hers and doing a side-by-side comparison with his.

"This is our only class together, but you have Calculus across from my Statistics class next period." He returned her schedule and flashed her that smile that made her insides turn to Jello.

"So?" She wasn't trying to be rude, but she wasn't sure what his point was.

"*So?*" He mimicked her, raising a brow. "I'll walk you to your next class."

"I think I can find my way," she said, returning her attention to her desk.

"I'm sure you can, but since we're going to the exact same place. I'll walk with you."

"Look," she began to let him down easy. "I'm not looking–"

"I'm not looking for anything either. I'm just trying to be nice. Have you never made friends with anyone before, *Joey*?"

The way he said her name had little butterflies fluttering in her stomach.

"Duncan and DuVall," the professor called out. "I understand you may not be related, but I'm sure you can find time to continue your introductions after class."

Shane flashed her a smirk before turning around.

A war raged inside Joey because part of her wanted him to like her and was giddy over his attention, but the other part reminded her of her grandmother's warning. The fact that he made her feel so weak in the knees was a clear-cut sign that she needed to steer clear of him. It wasn't her plan to not date guys at all, but she wasn't trying to get too serious with anyone.

A paper being slipped onto her desk pulled her out of her thoughts. If Shane was anything, it was persistent. She opened the note and had to tamp down a giggle. In true middle school fashion, he created a *Do you like me* note, but instead, he asked *Will you be my friend?* With one checkbox for Yes and one for Hell Yeah.

Joey couldn't help but smile as she underlined the word friend before checking Yes and slipping the letter over his shoulder when the teacher wasn't looking. Despite all her internal warnings, she relished the nostalgia and fun of passing notes in class with a cute boy. It's not like she wouldn't see him again in the gym when they were both at practice and all the games.

She also thought of all the stares and guys trying to get her attention as she walked to class and figured it would be nice to have a buffer. Joey was a stallion. Tall and thick with it. Her frame was very sturdy, with her legs and ass being the thickest part of her. Her crop top and leggings combo had guys trying to follow her across campus.

Sometimes, she wondered what it would be like to be slim like Kiko or an hourglass like Nicole, but only sometimes. For the most part, she was very proud of her thicker frame. She was fit and healthy, and the boys went crazy over her body. Looking at the back of Shane's head, his tattoo peaked out over the collar of his shirt, and it intrigued her.

What was the harm in being his friend?

So, for the next few weeks, they got to know each other during their walks from class to class and passed notes during English class. Shane was fun and thoughtful and somehow kept the other guys on the basketball team from bugging her and her friends. When he found out she worked at Dairy Queen, he and the rest of the team were guaranteed to come by at least once during her shift. Sometimes, they sat in there for a couple of hours after practice.

One night, near the end of her shift, her cell phone buzzed in her pocket. Getting calls was unusual for her, so she ignored it, thinking it was a wrong number. Then it happened again, ringing out two times back-to-back. It was against the rules to have her phone at the register, so she had to wait until she finished with her customer. When she went to the break room to check who it was, she found four missed calls from her grandmother's neighbor, Mrs. Pearl.

A sense of unease overcame Joey as she returned the call.

"Hello? Joey girl?"
"Hi, Mrs. Pearl. Is everything ok?"
"Naw, baby. I hate to tell you this way, but your Grann done passed. I was stoppin' by to pick up a bread she baked for me, but she didn't answer the door. I found her in the front room. She was still warm but gone."
"What?"
"They said you can claim her body when you get here. I'm just glad I found her when I did, before the 'mortis set in. I'm sorry, baby. You gotta come as soon as you can."

Joey didn't even remember ending the call. She could barely find the words to let her manager know she had to leave. It was dark when she stepped out into the quiet Tallahassee evening, and seeing the bus stop empty, she knew she most likely missed the bus, so she began the two-mile walk to her apartment. It didn't even register to her that it might not be safe or that she should call for a cab. The world around her was fuzzy and fading at the corners. It didn't even cross her mind to call her mother.

Halfway home, a group of guys began to cat-call her from across the street. She ignored them, not even looking up to count how many or see what they looked like. Her mind was so out of it she didn't even register the footsteps advancing on her.

"Hey," the strange male voice called to her. "I been tryna' talk to you."

Joey didn't reply or turn around. Her daze was that deep. To see her was reminiscent of a robot or the Terminator when he was focused on a mission. It wasn't until the guy grabbed her shoulder to get her attention that she totally cracked and began to scream.

"Don't touch me!" Joey screamed over and over. She was vaguely aware of other voices yelling as she fell to her knees. She curled up into a ball, the weight of the pain of her grandmother's death pressing down on her. Her tears broke, the sound of her tormented sobs sounding foreign to her own ears.

"Joey!" A loud voice broke through the haze as she felt her body being lifted up.

"Leave me alone," she cried out, fighting against whoever was touching her.

"Joey! It's me, *Shane!*" The familiar voice and use of her name calmed her somewhat. "Relax. We got you."

Joey felt her fear subside, but she began to shake uncontrollably.

"Help me put her in the car." Shane motioned to Jay, his teammate, to assist him with Joey, who was distressed. He had been driving past when he saw her screaming and some strange guy standing over her. Without thinking, Shane pulled over, jumped out of the car, and shoved the guy, who his other teammates then hemmed up. The way she was curled up on the ground, screaming with her eyes tightly closed, he could tell something was off.

Once they got her in the car, he tried to get her to talk.

"Joey? It's Shane. What happened?" He rubbed her back and arm to soothe her. Joey's eyes were finally open, but she looked scared and confused. "Are you ok?"

"I have to go home," she said, still somewhat dazed.

"Did that guy hurt you?"

"No." She shook her head furiously. "I just have to go home," she repeated, the tears beginning to stream again.

"Man, I didn't do nothin' to her," the guy yelled outside the car. "I just tapped her shoulder, and she started screaming her head off. I don't know what her problem is, but I ain't do nothin'."

The guys let him go, and he righted his clothes, storming away from the scene.

"Joey? Do you need to get back to the dorms? We can take you."

"I don't live on campus," she replied, finally calm enough to talk. "I have an apartment."

"Ok. So, I can take you there," Shane offered. "You guys wait for me at Dairy Queen. Let me get her straight, and then I'll come back."

"I'm rolling with you," Jay said. He was concerned that Joey might have another episode or breakdown.

"Cool," Shane replied. The two boys jumped in the front seat of his Chrysler 300, and then Shane turned back to look at Joey. "Where do you live?"

She sniffed before staring out her window. "In the Townsend Efficiencies."

Shane glanced at Jay, confused. "Where are those? I never heard of them."

"I think they're behind the Waffle House," Jay replied.

Shane glanced back to Joey, who simply nodded. Shrugging, he faced forward and pulled out into traffic. They weren't far from where she'd confirmed, and in a matter of minutes, he was turning into the rundown complex. He frowned in confusion about why she would be staying there but didn't say anything. Jay just shrugged and hopped out of the car, helping her out of the back seat. They followed behind her as she walked toward the first-level apartment. The inside was nice, but the exterior and neighborhood left a lot to be desired.

Once she was in her safe space, Joey didn't know what to do first. She dragged her suitcase out of the closet, but then the sadness consumed her again. Before she knew it, she was full-on crying in the middle of the room.

Shane and Jay were dumbfounded as they watched her meltdown. Shane looked to Jay, who shrugged and motioned for him to do something. Scratching his head and uncertain what to do, Shane stepped toward her.

"Joey? Talk to me. What happened?"
"My grandmother passed away," she sniffed. "I have to go home."

Understanding overcame Shane, and he immediately pulled her into a hug. "I'm so sorry, Joey."

"Yeah, Joey. I'm sorry to hear that," Jay said as he perched on the chair across from her bed.

Just then, her phone vibrated with another phone call. This time, it was her mother.

"Hello?" She could barely control the sob that wanted to break free.

"Joey? Did you hear about your Grann?"

"Yeah. Mrs. Pearl called to tell me. I'm packing to go home now."

"I knew she wasn't well, but I didn't expect this," her mother said tearfully.

"I just spoke to her a couple of days ago. She complained of a headache but said she was ok. When are you flying out?"

There was a long stretch of silence between them, during which time all she could hear was her mother sighing and sniffing.

"Well, I'll try to make the funeral. You know I don't have anyone to watch the kids, and I can't afford to bring them all with me."

"Mom," Joey replied unbelievingly. "You have to come. Who's gonna plan everything?"

"Well, Joey, you were closer to your grandmother. You can handle it. And like I said, I'll try to make the funeral."

"Try to make it? I can't plan a funeral! Oh my God," Joey cried out.

"Stop being so dramatic," her mother tossed back. "You know I can't just jump up and leave. The twins are both sick, and I don't know if their dad can –"

Her mother began to list out all the reasons why she might not be able to help plan or attend her own mother's funeral. Stunned, Joey flopped down on her hard mattress. She tuned out her mother's words as the weight of responsibility crashed down on her. The last thing on her mind was having to plan the funeral of the woman she loved most in the world. Her body began to rock as she tried to keep herself from breaking down.

Kneeling to look her face-to-face, Shane took the phone dangling loosely in her hand. He hung up the call, with no protest from Joey, and tossed the phone by her purse, placing both hands on her shoulder to get her full attention.

"How can I help?"
"Yeah," Jay chimed in. "We can help you with your plane tickets, pack, or whatever."
"Do you need money for your flight?"
"No, I got that. I just don't know how I'm supposed to deal with all of this," she said, dazed.
"Do you have any aunts or uncles that can help? Anyone?"
She let out a heavy sigh. "No. My mother is an only child. All my grandmother's siblings have already passed on. There are a few distant relatives, but no one that I've even seen in years. Our neighbor found her."

She began to cry at the thought of Grann dying and no one being there to help her. She wondered how long she'd been lying there before Mrs. Pearl found her. Just the thought that she'd go back to that little blue house and her grandmother wouldn't be in it, would never be in it again, broke her heart. Her hands flew to her face as she tried to conceal the ugly cry that tore through her.

"It will be ok." Shane tried to comfort her. He couldn't imagine going through what she was about to do alone, and he sat next to her and pulled her into his embrace. He hugged her while he thought of a way to help her.

"I can come with you if you want." He suggested.

"You can't do that," she cried. "What about school?"

"Death in the family? They already swear we're related as it is."

That made Joey chuckle despite her sadness. "Really? You would come with me?"

"Yeah. I have no idea what needs to be done, but at least you won't have to do it alone. Your grandmother is in Louisiana, right? I have an aunt who lives in Baton Rouge. She'll come help us if I ask."

"Are you for real? That would be amazing." The amount of hope she felt at that moment was unlike anything she'd ever felt.

"Yep. You pack. I'll take care of the tickets and call my aunt."

"Thank you," Joey cried. She threw her arms around him and returned one of the best hugs she'd ever received in her life.

Chapter 2

After dinner, they strolled back to the hotel. Nicole was up for the walk but knew she didn't have it in her for much more and wanted to extend the time with her friends. The couples parted ways once they reached the corner of the street where the Bulgari Hotel Milano was located. The night was still young, and Joey wanted to get Shane a fruit tart from a bakery they had passed on their way back from the yacht. They linked arms as they strolled down the quaint street lined with designer boutiques, cafés, and a mixture of modern and old-world architecture.

"I think I see why Nicole fell in love with being here. The vibes are so romantic," Joey sighed.

"I think Nicole fell in love with Jay. She would be smitten with any city he was in. They could be in Timbuktu, and she'd be happy."

They both laughed. "You might have a point."

Joey considered that statement for a moment. Maybe she was feeling what she was feeling because she was with Shane because it was always love whenever they were together. The more time they spent around each other, the more at peace she felt. Her only concern was that they couldn't seem to find that contentment anywhere else or with anyone else.

"Shit," Shane grunted, pulling her out of her thoughts.
"What happened?"
"Guy across the street, he recognized me and has a camera."

Before she could blink, Shane gripped her around the waist and spun them both down a side alley, which happened to be the side entrance to a bakery. He peeked around the corner and quickly ducked back beside her, swearing under his breath.

"I guess it was too much to think I could enjoy myself out here and go unnoticed."
"Well, considering you're damn near seven feet tall and brown..."

He looked down at her and grinned as a short, stout Italian woman with salt and pepper hair shuffled out the door. She was startled, not expecting to see two people standing outside and two people who were clearly not from there. Her fright quickly warmed to curiosity as she looked them over, taking in what seemed to be a lover's embrace since Shane's arm was still around Joey's waist. A knowing smile spread across her face as she threw her arms out and began to tut something in Italian.

"Shhh," Shane playfully hushed her, placing a finger over his mouth before gesturing across the street. Waddling to the alley's entrance, she glanced around until she saw the photographer poised and ready to shoot with his camera. She nodded in understanding before pushing her vendor cart to block the entrance.

"*Grazie*," Shane said as he bowed his head to her in thanks. "*Lo sono Shane e lei è Joey.*"

"*Mi Antanella*," she replied, gesturing to herself. "Come." She strode back into the doorway, prompting them to follow her into what turned out to be a bakery and a cozy restaurant kitchen. The decadent aroma of baking bread and pasta assaulted Joey, a foodie at heart.

"Is it wrong that we just ate dinner, but I could totally crush whatever she's cooking?"
"Nah, 'cause I feel the same way. I wonder what it is?" Shane looked around before engaging their host in a crude exchange of Italian to go along with her broken English. He'd learned the language from his international scrimmages. Joey was just able to make out that there was Ziti in the oven.

"Ooh! Ask her if she has any fruit tarts."

"Hai qualche crostata di frutta?" The deepness of his voice communicating in a different language had a slow heat creeping up Joey's spine.

"Ah, sí! Vieni a vedere," the woman said as she led them to the front of the shop, where all the pastries were on display in a glass case.

"Oh, *yes*," Joey moaned as she took in the variety of fresh desserts. Shane was preoccupied with looking out the shop window to see if he could locate the paparazzi.

"Posso?" He asked, tentatively holding up the open sign and turning it to closed. He pulled out a wad of money, suggesting he'd compensate her for closing her shop early.

"No, no, no," she shook her head in furious denial.

"Insisto," Shane argued, pointing at Joey. *"Mangerà tutto!"*

Antonella laughed and grudgingly accepted the money, flashing them a megawatt smile as she sauntered over to the counter and put the cash in an old-school mechanical register. She began to hum a song as she counted the bills and placed them in a special receptacle before washing her hands and drying them against her red gingham apron before returning to the kitchen.

"What did you say?" Joey was curious how he convinced her.

"I told her you were going to eat everything," he laughed.

"Shane!" Joey punched him in the arm playfully as she giggled. "You ain't lying, though. Everything looks so good. I wanna taste a little of the Ziti, some of that fresh crusty bread, and then this tarte has my name all over it," she said, pointing to a specific dessert topped with fresh strawberries and kiwi.

"I'm gonna have to roll ya ass outta here, huh?"

"As long as you roll me back to the hotel, I don't care," she laughed.

"Come," Antonella gestured all around. "You eat?"

"*Grazi*," Joey said gratefully as she pointed toward the baked pasta on a cooling rack.

"I think this is actually a bed and breakfast," Shane noted as he examined the menu. He'd roamed around the shop, closed all the blinds, and locked the front door.

"Seriously?"

"Yeah," he said, confirming with Antonella. "She says there are four rooms upstairs."

Joey nodded as they both exchanged a knowing look.

"You wanna check it out?" Shane arched a brow as he awaited her response.

"Sure."

To Joey's delight, the bed and breakfast decor was surprisingly modern compared to the rustic setup of the eatery below. The back hallway and staircase were a buffed and polished olive wood with chrome accents that instantly transported them into a designer boutique-inspired home as they followed Antonella up to the second level.

She showed them three rooms, each featuring luxurious queen-sized beds with opulent bedding and furniture. The last room was the largest, boasting a king-sized bed and a large wooden armoire. The remaining furniture, including a couch, desk, and freestanding vanity mirror, was stark white in contrast with the warm burgundy bedding.

"This is so charming," Joey said in wonder. "I would have never guessed all this was up here based on the little restaurant below."

"I guess that's why you're not supposed to judge a book by its cover," Shane shrugged, raising his brows. Joey rolled her eyes, knowing he was referring to more than just the room.

"You like?" Antonella eyed them wickedly as she began to prep the room.

Shane stood with his legs spread and hands behind his back as they waited for Joey's response. He watched her intently as she looked around the room, stalling so she didn't seem as eager as she was to say yes. He knew her so well.

"There's a dope-ass entertainment system and a TV. We could eat and order as many desserts as you want," Shane cajoled her.

"And nice tub," Antonella added, motioning to the large jacuzzi spa as she opened up wooden shutters that led to the bathroom. "And I make good breakfast."

"Sold!" Joey laughed as she peered out the window at the view of the lake in the distance.

"Good! I will bring food." Antonella smiled proudly as she opened the closet and laid two luxurious robes across the bed before heading downstairs to prepare their plates.

Joey finally glanced at Shane, who wore a satisfied smirk. "You're real funny."

"What? Don't act like you didn't want to stay the minute you saw the room and thought about all the treats you could eat."

"Whatever," she laughed. "Well, I guess we haven't had a sleepover in a while."

She plopped into a plush high-back chair and observed Shane while he explored the room. It was Kiko's wedding when she had made the decision that they focus on being friends and ending the sexual side of their relationship, consisting of a handful of encounters, especially after meeting Dante. Shane wasn't happy with her decision, and it caused tension between them until they saw each other at Nicole's birthday weekend and discovered how much they missed each other. She missed the fun and playful side of their bond.

Joey was in an open relationship with Dante, allowing her to indulge her deep affection for Shane without feeling guilty—well, not *too* guilty. Shane's relationship with Kelly made it easy for her to evade his advances. The problem was that they couldn't ignore their feelings when they were around each other, and when he had suggested they meet in Italy for his birthday, she had a feeling it would lead to them crossing the line.

"It'll be fun. Want to make a bet on how long that paparazzi guy will wait before he gives up on getting the pic?" Shane stood by the window, peeking through the Roman blinds at the shop across the street.

"Oh my God! Is he still out there?"

"Yeah, he's been waiting at the bar across the street."

"Damn. He really wants that picture. I kinda feel bad for him."

Shane glared at her like she was crazy. "Man... Fuck him." He threw up his middle finger at the window. "Tryna' catch me out there. Will you still feel bad for him when your face is plastered everywhere, and they start calling you a homewrecker?"

"Point taken."

"You know, we wouldn't have to worry about all that if you would just break up wit yo boring ass man friend."

"I'd still be a homewrecker until you break it off with Kelly, so..."

"You know her time is almost up," Shane replied soberly.

"Ok... well, when it's all the way up, we'll talk."

Shane groaned in frustration.

"No one told you to go and do that stupid shit in the first place."

"My *publicist* suggested I get a girlfriend to curb the rumors that I was a womanizer."

"True. But your *publicist* did not tell you to draft a three-year contract with a woman you can barely tolerate. What made you choose Kelly anyway?"

He shrugged. "She was sweet. At least she was when we dated in high school."

Joey rolled her eyes and shook her head as she slipped off her shoes and got comfortable. She remembered how Kelly used to call him every night before bed during their freshman year. As much as Shane complained about her, she had always been around. It was another reason Joey didn't take him too seriously.

Deciding to change the subject, she focused on the vibe.

"Ooh! Let's see what new playlist Chelle has up."

She scrolled until she found one that she felt would set the mood. "Lovers and Friends" by Lil Jon featuring Usher came streaming through the hidden surround sound speakers. Shane bopped his head to the music as he walked toward her and then perched on the edge of the bed near her chair. He pulled one of her legs onto his lap to massage her feet. She'd been a trooper and didn't complain when Nicole decided to walk instead of taking his arranged car service to their dinner, but he knew those five-inch heels versus cobblestone couldn't have been comfortable.

"Ah, thank you," she sighed. "But back to your bad decision. You could have waited before you made Kelly sign on the dotted line, or at least do a year trial. Now you're stuck."

"Yeah. And she's been hinting about us continuing things after the time is up."

"Are you serious?"

He leveled her with a severe frown, and she sighed.

"You can't be mad at me on my birthday," he sighed in return.

"I'm not mad," she replied just as Antonella returned with a cart carrying their baked ziti, a bottle of champagne, and an array of desserts. The bottom compartment housed a few more bottles of bubbly and an assortment of wine. She took in the sight of Shane rubbing Joey's ankles and smiled.

"I bring all you need," she managed in her broken English. "You can use kitchen if you want."

"*Grazi*," Shane replied as he stood and walked her to the door, pulling another wad of bills from his money clip. It was enough to cover her overhead for the next month, but she took it without protest, smiling even brighter at the lovely American couple.

"Buona notte!" She waved at Joey, who was already tinkering with the food trays, before closing the door behind her.

"Are you really about to eat a second dinner?"

"Please. That dinner was five stars, but the portions were baby-sized. I know Nicole ordered room service when she got back to her room."

Shane laughed. "She probably did. But she's also eating for two."

"Shut the hell up and stop acting like your ass ain't about to tear up this pasta," she said as she put a forkful in her mouth. *"Mmm.* So good!"

"It does look good as hell," he noted.

"Hmm." She offered him a forkful. Shane maintained eye contact as he opened his mouth and allowed her to feed him. The groan that rumbled from his throat proved he was thoroughly satisfied. "Good, right?"

"That's delicious. Damn," he moaned.

"I aspire to cook this good when I grow up," Joey joked.

"You're a pretty damn good cook. But if you can make this? I'd love you forever."

Joey laughed. "You already gotta love me forever, *bestie.*"

"Don't call me that." He grimaced.

"What's wrong with it?"

"Bestie," he grumbled. "Like I'm some simp in the friend zone."

"Oh, please. You know that's not the case."

"Isn't it, though? I'm your bestie while you shack up with Dante."

"Well, *bestie*, you were the one who said I wasn't relationship material."

"That's not what I said."

"My bad. I'm not *traditional* wife material." She corrected using air quotes.

"Why do you say it like that's not what you always say about yourself? You're a self-proclaimed free spirit. Are you not?"

"Yes. Until I'm ready to settle down. But I'm never gonna be a stay-at-home only wife, and that's what you're looking for. Am I wrong?"

There was a moment of silence as the music drifted between them. "Here I Stand" by Usher was like Shane had a background singer doing his dirty work. There were so many unsettled emotions between them. She was scared to be without him but scared to lose him as a friend. He wanted more, but was she ready?

"You're not wrong. I guess," Shane sighed heavily.

"I feel like I'm walking into a trap," Joey groaned, leaning forward. "What's the long sigh for?"

"You know what it is." He looked her in the eyes, hoping she understood his seriousness. He'd already told her how he felt.

"Shane... What do you want me to do?"

"Break up with Dante," he said firmly.

"And then?"

"Be with me? What do you mean?"

"You make it sound so easy. Right now, you're in Arizona, and I'm in Cali. Not to mention, you are always on the road. And, oops, I forgot Kelly."

"Kelly isn't a factor, and you know it. And, as far as my team, let's work on getting me to L.A. My contract is almost up with Phoenix, so it's the perfect time."

"Well, we can talk when you break up with your girlfriend."

"I wanna talk now. We're both here. Face to face," he said, leaning closer. "I want you, Joey. Do you want me?"

His voice deepened to its lowest register, which did crazy things to her insides. She looked away, unable to stand the intensity in his eyes. Unable to formulate her thoughts because all she could think and feel was him. It was already hard enough to deny him anything, but she needed to be more careful when it came to her freedom. The thought of them ruining their friendship because they tried to be something they weren't, terrified her.

"Joey," he breathed out, placing one of his long fingers under her chin and tipping her face back toward him. "Do you want me?"

The way Shane's voice was gentle yet firm, but the expression in his eyes was fiercely serious, made her breath hitch. Her heart detonated in her chest as all the emotions she kept hidden deep inside begged to be released. There was only one possible answer to everything she was feeling.

"Yes," she uttered in a shallow whisper. She felt like she had just breathed her first breath. Shane cupped her cheek, stroking her bottom lip with his thumb. She held his hand to her face, turned into his palm, and kissed it. He slid off the bed, kneeling in between her legs and resting his head on her lap, his hands wrapping around her thighs.

"I love you," he uttered.
"I love you, too," Joey rasped on the verge of tears. Shane was her whole heart, but the desire to be with him was as strong as the fear of losing him. She ran her fingers through his tight curls that he let grow out into a tapered fro while he kissed his way up her thighs through the smooth fabric of her skirt. He kept going up the center of her torso until he was able to nestle his face between her breasts, placing kisses against her heart.

"I'm scared, Shane," Joey admitted.

Shane continued to plant a trail of soft kisses until he reached her neck, which he nuzzled, savoring her scent. Then he slid his fingers through her coils and undid the tie that kept them contained.

"I need you," he whispered against her ear, pressing his lips to her temple. His arms slid around her shoulders to rest on the back of the chair, pinning her in.

"I know you're scared, Shawty, but I won't hurt you," he said as he pressed his lips to hers. "I promise."

Joey exhaled with a shudder, wrapping her arms around his neck and leaning into his kiss. It was soft and tender, the way she loved it. Well, that's how they always started, with him gently coaxing his way into her mouth and licking her tongue. Soon, it morphed into the flames of their need for each other. Staying away wasn't easy, so the tension was thick when they were around each other.

Shane gathered Joey up in one dramatic swoop in his long, strong arms and playfully tossed her on the bed.

"Shane!" Her giggles rang out until he began to strip, similar to when he'd danced for her at the joint bachelor/bachelorette party at Kiko's wedding. She watched him through lowered lids as he undid his cufflinks and slowly unbuttoned his shirt.

"You like watching me?"

His raspy voice boomed as his eyes held hers. Joey simply smirked as she crawled up on her knees, kissing his tattoo-covered chest as she began to undo his belt. He'd started with two in college, and now he was almost completely covered from his neck to his ankles. It was just a form of self-expression to him, but the media had projected a bad boy image on him after one fight and dating two popular influencers. Now, everything he did was considered borderline scandalous.

Shane leaned down, kissing her neck and nipping her ear before dragging his lips to hers and snaking his tongue into her mouth. Joey moaned deeply, and he groaned in response, his urgency increasing as he shoved his shirt off and then grasped the hem of her dress and pushed it up.

Joey nuzzled and licked his torso, the path traveling south toward his open zipper. Shane grunted when she reached into his boxer briefs, grasped his erection and pulled it free. He watched her intently as she stroked it from root to tip before placing her lips to the head for a gentle kiss. She looked him in the eyes as she began to swallow his length.

"That's it, baby," he encouraged her as she took him to the back of her throat and moaned. Slipping his fingers through her hair, he gradually tightened his grip, holding her steady. She constricted her throat muscles around his length before pulling back and repeating the motion until he groaned.

"Let me fuck your face."

Placing a hand on each side of her head, he pulled his hips back as she hollowed her cheeks, then thrust forward until he was touching the back of her throat. They found a rhythm until all that was heard was Joey's slurping and slight gagging when he pushed just past her limits, which she loved. Shane was the only man that she'd ever trusted completely, sexually. He'd proven she could trust him to let her explore her darkest desires without judgment or scrutiny.

Shane hung his head back as he enjoyed the hot suction of Joey's mouth. Just like he knew her, she understood him. Oral sex was his favorite, giving *and* receiving. When his fingers began to flex and grasp the strands of her hair, she maneuvered her body so that she laid on her back with her head hanging off the side of the bed and let her legs fall open. He leaned forward, hitching her skirt up further around her hips until her lace thong was exposed. Slipping a finger underneath, he found her juices flowing.

"Damn, I missed this super-soaker," he murmured. He slid two fingers into her pussy, thrusting just to feel the slickness.

Joey lifted her hips, chasing the friction of his touch. When his thumb began to flick her clit, she let out a needy whine. She wanted to feel him thrusting deep inside of her, but she also loved having him in her mouth.

"I can't wait to taste you," he panted.

Gripping her firmly with one hand under her back and the other under her ass, he lifted her so that she was upside down and her pussy was in his face. Joey rested her knees on his shoulder as he smashed his face into her center. She began to grind against him, already feeling that wild heat uncoiling within her, and sucked him with the same ferocious vigor. Shane's hips began to buck with the intense pleasure.

"Keep sucking me just like that," he instructed.

When it felt like his knees might buckle, he switched their position again so that she was on her back as he hovered over her. Once she adjusted, he began to thrust into her mouth at a steady pace, chasing his mounting release. He spread her thighs wide as he suckled and laved her clit while his two fingers thrust into her slick canal and his pinky rimmed her backdoor.

"Mmm," she moaned wildly as her legs began to shake, and her climax fractured her into what felt like a million pieces. Hearing her cries as she continued to suck and gag around his shaft sent Shane over the edge with her. Careful not to crush her, he pistoned his hips until his cum was bursting in hot spurts down her throat. Joey was a pro and didn't break stride until he was done shaking and jerking and collapsed beside her.

"Come here," he called to her.

Weakly, she managed to crawl up the bed until she curled into his embrace. He pulled her closer, kissing her forehead and the tip of her nose before placing a gentle kiss on her lips, rolling on top of her to deepen the intensity. The gentleness of his touch incited a frenzy within her, and soon, she was grasping at him, shoving his pants all the way off while he peeled away her clothing.

"I missed you," he uttered hoarsely against her lips. "I don't want to be without you anymore. I can't."

Joey simply moaned in response. In her fantasies, in a perfect world, she could imagine her and Shane together. She could see him as a loving father and husband—the dream house, the lavish lifestyle they had dreamed up in his dorm room.

"What if we don't work? What happens to us then?"

"We make it work, Joey. That's not an option," he breathed against her shoulder as he continued to remove her clothes.

"And what about Kelly?"

Shane nudged Joey's legs open wider, sucking on her neck as he lined his shaft at her entrance. She gasped as he plunged into her to the hilt. Looking so deep into her eyes that her soul felt seen. He raised her hands above her head and entwined his fingers with hers as he began to deep-stroke her.

"Forget about Kelly."

Joey's fingers gripped his as she arched into his rough thrusts. The way he was rocking her body into submission had her ready to lose her mind and forget all the shit from their past. But some things were harder than others.

"You love fuckin' me," she uttered as she looked up into his eyes. Shane's eyes blinked slowly, her words hitting their mark as he fought not to lose control.

"You know I love this pussy," he replied through his teeth.

"But I'm not wifey material," she tossed out, not quite over him saying those words to her, even if he had apologized.

"Why are you fuckin' with me?" Shane grunted as he slowed down his pace to gently ease in and out of her. He pushed their hands together, pinning hers above her head with one hand while the other slid down to caress her face.

"I never meant that, Joey. Even when the words left my mouth, my heart knew it was bullshit. You know that."

Joey's eyes stung as tears threatened to form. Her throat tightened with emotion, and she turned her head away. Even though she wanted to believe his words, it was difficult to accept his offer. She knew she was in her head about it because her heart was ready to forgive him, and her body already had.

"Don't turn away from me, baby," he whispered as he nudged her with his nose before kissing her ear. "Look at me."

Joey did as he said and met his determined gaze. "I promise I'll never hurt you again."

Chapter 3

October 2010 (Nicole's birthday weekend)

"C'mon, guys! We don't have much time before Nicole gets back."

Kiko clapped her hands as she rushed her friends to finish putting up the pink, white, and gold decorations for Nicole's birthday surprise. Joey was arranging the two-layer birthday cake with just one candle in the center of the kitchen table. Across the room, Shane was taping the balloons to the wall as his girlfriend, Kelly, handed them to him.

There was tension between the three of them, well, between Kelly and Joey, because Kelly had always been wary of how close Shane was to Joey, and Joey couldn't understand why he kept Kelly around. Being an honest, straight shooter, Shane was upfront about how important Joey was to him and how often they spoke. Even though their relationship was part of a contract deal to help him clean up his image, Kelly felt it was enough to build on and pick up where they left off in high school. She felt that choosing her for the job meant something.

Kelly also knew that Shane had met up with Joey after his game in L.A. a few weeks prior, and it was no secret that Joey sometimes flew out to watch him play on the road. She used her role as his publicist as a buffer to downplay their relationship. The fact that she played a considerable part in diminishing the bad boy image he'd acquired explained her vested interest in him versus her other clients. Kelly complained that she knew there was more to those visits than just work.

And she was right.

The truth was that ever since they graduated, reality had been a cold slap in the face. Living on campus meant seeing each other almost daily, but that bubble burst when Joey moved to Los Angeles and Shane was drafted to Phoenix. It was their first time apart since they met freshman year, and Shane wasn't handling it well. That, and the fact that Joey started dating Dante as soon as she moved to Cali and eventually moved in with him.

The partying, tattoos, and aggressive behavior on the court had been the result, even though Joey didn't realize it at the time.

When she found out about the contract with Kelly, she could have killed Shane. He claimed he was following her instructions to find a nice girl to help his image, which required a contract. Joey thought he was just trying to one-up her since she was with Dante. The problem was that Kelly took her role seriously, and Shane had to act accordingly. In the meantime, Shane and Joey's feelings for each other became increasingly apparent, but they couldn't do anything without causing him more scandal.

So, they crept around.

Dante was also suspicious of their relationship, but he didn't complain much due to his open status with Joey. And, she did a great job of keeping her movements under wraps because her life, or livelihood at least, literally depended on it. It was with Dante's help that she landed her job at one of the leading PR agencies on the West Coast. Her stacked clientele didn't hurt either.

Dante entered the kitchen after finishing a work call and slid his arm around Joey. Both Chelle and Remy, who had double-dated with the couple a few times, greeted him warmly. Kiko, who'd suggested they hook up, gave him a hug, Kelly a stiff wave, and Shane dapped him up. There was an awkward silence until Kiko announced that Nicole had just pulled into the driveway.

"Shhh! Everyone, come on this side of the table," Kiko whispered as she pulled out her camera phone to capture the moment. Everyone positioned themselves accordingly, and Shane just so happened to wind up on the other side of Joey. She giggled, anticipating Nicole's response to them all being there, and he pinched her waist to be quiet. Joey all but jumped out of her skin from his touch but said nothing.

"You got the chills, babe?" Dante rubbed the goosebumps that had sprouted up on her arm.
"I'll be fine."

"Lucy! I'm home," Nicole yelled from the living room, to which Kiko replied, "I'm in the kitchen!"

Shane's hand had dropped to his side, but his fingers were tracing a random pattern from Joey's hips to her ass. Dante's arm was around her, so if she tried to push Shane's hand away, it would bring attention to the issue. If she looked up at Shane, someone would see it, so she stood there, her pussy roaring to life as he teased her.

She shifted on her feet, flashing a fake smile up at Dante when he looked down on her with concern.

When Nicole burst into the kitchen and everyone yelled "Happy Birthday," Shane grabbed a handful of her ass. Joey kicked his leg, but that just caused him to tighten his grip.

When Nicole's shock wore off, Joey used that opportunity to slink out of Dante's embrace and elbow Shane in the side before making her way to her friend to hug her.

After that, she tried her best to stay away from him. She breathed a sigh of relief when the guys, minus Dante, who had business to do, decided to go to the campus to check out the Homecoming festivities. It gave her a chance to catch up with her girls and breathe without Shane or his weird-ass girlfriend breathing down her neck.

She was sitting out on the patio after Chelle presented Nicole with her first birthday gift, her signed divorce papers, after finally tracking down her husband, Trey. She'd just explained her friendship with Shane as just that, and played up his newly formed reputation as a ladies' man when she received a text.

> Stalk: I miss you
> Juicy: You just saw me
> Stalk: I mean it. This is killing me
> Juicy: What is?
> Stalk: Not having you in my bed every night
> Stalk: Not waking up to you every day
> Juicy: Where is all this coming from?
> Stalk: Kelly was a mistake

Joey was stunned. It was shocking to see him be so vulnerable. They had always been playful, with moments of deep conversations mixed in, but he was her rock. He'd never been needy, clinging, or possessive of her.

That night, when the guys returned, Jay asked Joey and Shane to help him set up something special to cheer Nicole up. They decorated his room with candles throughout and rose petals. The music and ambiance were relaxing and sexy, courtesy of one of Chelle's playlists. By the time they finished, Shane tried to sneak a kiss by the staircase, but approaching footsteps caused them to break apart and head in different directions.

Joey felt it was safest to go to her room, where Dante was conducting a call with clients on the West Coast. She took a nice hot shower and then curled up in bed with the latest Zane novel she'd picked up for her flight. When Dante was done with his call, he breathed a long sigh. He crawled onto the bed next to her, barely able to explain the details of his call to her before dozing off.

Unable to sleep, Joey updated her social media with pictures of the crew from earlier that night. When her phone vibrated with a message, she was almost afraid to check it. She knew it would be Shane, but she opened it on the off chance it was one of the girls.

> Stalk: Meet me out back
> Juicy: I'm in the bed!
> Stalk: I need to talk to you. Important
> Juicy: No you don't! Lol
> Stalk: C'mon! Don't make me beg!
> Juicy: Go on...
> Stalk: Joey...
> Stalk: please.

Holding back a deep sigh, Joey waited a few seconds before sliding out of the bed. Dante was snoring, so she knew he wasn't going to budge. It was ridiculous to entertain Shane, but for some absurd reason, she had a hard time telling him no. A part of her also missed him like crazy; she always felt like she was missing a part of herself when they were apart. She tried to chalk it up to the nostalgia of being back in their old stomping grounds, but the feeling had been building up in her for a while. And every time they were around each other, she felt the pull to be close to him.

Sneaking out of her room and down the stairs, she found the house still. Soft music drifted from Chelle and Remy's room, and she knew Jay and Nicole would be occupied. Kiko was in her room, so there was no one to question what she was doing. She entered the kitchen and saw Shane waiting outside the sliding glass door. Her feet pushed forward with intrigue on what he had to say.

"Hey, you," he said softly, caressing her cheek with his finger.
"Hey," she whispered. "I'm here. What's so important?"

Shane held her smaller hand in his, examining it like he'd never seen a hand before.

"You. You're important, Joey. I fucked up."

"What does that mean?"

"That whole bullshit about 'what my wife should be like' and my type. None of that shit matters. I love you. You in my life is what matters to me."

Joey was unsure of how to feel as she absorbed his words. Her stomach dropped even as her heart fluttered with joy. Such a weird ass feeling. She couldn't decide if she should be excited or terrified.

Before she could even question him, he was on her. Shane pulled her into his arms, and in an instant, his mouth was glued to hers. He inhaled a sharp breath as if he couldn't breathe without her, and Joey shuddered with latent desire. One hand tangled in her hair, gripping it tight as he angled her head so that he could devour her neck. Joey tried to hold back her moans as his lips and teeth titillated her skin.

"I hate you so bad," she panted, even though it was the furthest thing from the truth. His hands were traversing her body like he hadn't touched her in years.

"I hate that your ass be in my dreams every night," he breathed against her cheek before kissing her again. His tongue pilfered her mouth, taking, sucking, and licking until Joey felt delirious.

"Why do you do this to me?" She gasped and clawed at his back.

"Because this is how you make me feel. Just by looking at you. Just by being in the same room as you."

His hand pulled up her T-shirt, gripped her breast, and tweaked her nipple before bending down to suction his lips around it. The heat of his mouth and the soft bite of his teeth had her quivering in his arms. Her hands were grasping the waistband of his jeans as she teased him by letting her fingers glide over his erection.

Voices coming from the kitchen caused them to freeze. Shane picked her up off her feet and moved around to what he figured to be the empty room with Nicole's things. Shane pushed her up against the door, desperate to finish what they started. They didn't even hear the door click before it slid open, revealing Jay and Nicole looking at them like they were crazy. Joey almost fell inside, and Jay had to catch her before she hit the ground.

"Whoa," Jay said as he steadied her. "What the hell are y'all doing?"

"Shhh," Shane said frantically as he stepped inside, slid the door shut, and closed the blinds.

"What in the world?" Nicole looked at the time and frowned; it was two o'clock in the morning. Before she could ask another question, she heard Kelly's muffled voice outside calling out for Shane.

"Jay, I need to holla at you. Come with me outside right quick," Shane said as if everything was perfectly normal.

Joey watched as Jay pulled on a shirt and left with Shane. Looking around the room, it was clear they'd walked in on the tail end of a wild time. She and Nicole stood there staring at each other for a moment until they both burst into laughter. Joey knew that things were getting messy and wondered how she was going to fix it.

Chapter 4

Joey sauntered down the hall from the conference room to her office on her five-inch stilettos, victory coursing through her veins. She'd just secured two more NFL players on her roster, compliments of Dom's referral. Not that she needed the help because her name and reputation were heavy in the streets. Most people had no idea how important it was for certain celebrities to curate a good image or just how much of a mess some of those same celebrities were behind the scenes.

Trent, one of Dom's teammates, was a prime example. He'd been placed on probation by the team and in danger of being dropped because of a video that hit the internet of him in a physical altercation with the mother of his children. Well, one of them, at least. The total count was now four baby mamas and six kids.

This particular mama was none other than Letty, the one who had crashed his date with Nicole a few years back. Even though he was defending himself, it was still a bad look to see him manhandle her so roughly as he attempted to stop her from setting his car on fire. There wasn't enough community service in the world to cover up all of his relationship drama. Still, Joey devised a strategy to help him clean up his image so that another team would pick him up for the next season.

Opening the door to her office, She was assaulted with the fragrance of a dozen bouquets of red and white roses placed all around her office, along with various gift boxes from her favorite designers. Her heart fluttered, and a smile spread across her face because she already knew who they were from by the fancy gold foil of the gift cards. It was the private delivery service that Shane used whenever he sent her something. Walking over to the most significant arrangement, centered on her desk, she snatched the card from its gold-plated holder and ripped the seal.

Juicy,
There aren't enough gifts in the world to express how much you mean to me. And even though you claim you don't like to make a big deal of your birthday, I know your spoiled ass loves presents.

Love you for life,
Shane

Joey laughed at the nickname, and she could feel the nostalgia creeping in. Their college years had been some of the best times of her life, her memories holding a magical quality whenever she thought back to everything they'd experienced together. No matter what happened, she could always count on him to have her back and help her smile through it.

Calling her Juicy was his bat signal. She'd made herself scarce since their trip to Italy, ignoring his push for them to become official. After the trip, she'd had to put out a few social media fires for him, one being a woman from Phoenix who claimed he was the father of her two-year-old son. She was lying, of course, but the fact he knew how these groupies got down yet continued to hang out with the "crowd" was infuriating. How was she supposed to take him seriously when it seemed he didn't take himself seriously?

After corralling a couple of the interns to help her get all her gifts to her car, Joey shut down her computer for the day. Everyone kept stopping by her office-turned-flower shop to admire the considerable amount of roses that had been delivered throughout the day. Most assumed they were from Dante, who was out of the country for business, and she just let them. It wasn't their business anyway.

Stepping out of the office building, she held the door open for the interns to push the cart with the gifts through when she spotted a driver standing in front of a limo with heavily tinted windows, holding up another bouquet of roses.

"Ms. DuVall?" The man said as he handed her the arrangement. "My name is Philip, and I'll be your driver for the evening. I can place your items in the trunk while you get settled in. There's a glass of your favorite white wine waiting for you. Happy birthday."

"Wow, Ms. DuVall. I wanna be like you when I grow up," one of the interns whispered in awe behind her.

Slightly flustered and overcome by Shane's surprise, Joey almost forgot anyone else was with her. She instructed them to get back to work before turning to her driver.

"Joey," she introduced herself. "Thank you, Philip."

"My pleasure," he said as he opened the door to the back of the limo.

When she slid into the plush leather seat, she half expected to find more flowers, but only the chilled bottle of Gewürztraminer wine awaited her. She poured a healthy glass before settling back into her seat as Philip loaded her packages. Once done, he slid into the driver's seat and turned to face her.

"We should arrive at your destination in about an hour and a half. Would you like to stop anywhere before we get on the highway?"

"No, I'm good. Thanks."

Philip nodded and then closed the privacy divider. Once he started the car, music played softly through the Bose speakers. Joey recognized Chelle's Quiet Storm playlist when a few of her favorite songs played back-to-back. Sipping her drink, she zoned out to "I'm Still Waiting" by Jodeci. Between the wine, the music, and the thought of where she was going, a warm haze overcame her body.

The length of the car ride cued her in that he was most likely driving her to Laguna Beach, to the beach house. It had been a few years since she'd been there, the last time being a surprise party Shane held for Jay's twenty-forth birthday. Joey and Shane would meet up there from time to time when he first joined the league, and the media frenzy around him was at its height.

It was still hard for her to fathom that Shane was an NBA star. The third overall pick of his draft class, he was in high demand because of his well-rounded skill set. He'd grown an additional two inches since freshman year and was a force to be reckoned with on the court. His ability to handle the ball like it was an extension of his aura and sharp defensive skills made him an invaluable asset. His looks and unique fashion sense were a hit with the fans, especially the ladies.

Joey kept her distance because she couldn't afford to be caught up in his dating drama while she made a name for herself. Paparazzi followed him everywhere, and everyone he was seen with became media fodder. Shane said he understood, but his resulting behavior said otherwise. He had adopted an almost arrogant, "I don't give a fuck" attitude when it came to the media and began partying and drinking.

That was where his troubles began. Shane wasn't a player, and even though he was used to attention from the ladies on campus as one of FAMU's star players, that was nothing compared to the volume of women coming at him once he went pro. He wasn't an asshole, though, and being "nice" had come back to bite him in the ass a few times. It took both Jay and Joey to help him navigate the groupies and create a protocol to keep him out of the gossip blogs.

That's when Joey demanded Shane clean up his image, and he'd gotten the bright idea to put Kelly under contract. Just thinking about it pissed her off, and she poured another glass of wine. She was tired of cleaning up his mess and playing her part behind the scenes. It wouldn't be a problem if they were just friends, but continuing to court her so aggressively made everything confusing.

As the car pulled up to the tall gates of the mansion, she fingered the diamond-studded bracelet that Dante had given her for her birthday. It was like the two men were working in tandem, attacking her from each side. As soon as Shane expressed his desire to be serious, Dante began hinting that he was ready to take their relationship to the next level.

Joey sighed as she waited for Philip to open her door. The cool, ocean-scented breeze helped to clear her mind. She wanted to enjoy her birthday but also had to make sense of her life. She loved and would always love Shane, but the timing wasn't right. Her career was on the line right along with her heart.

The massive ornate wooden doors to the house swung open, revealing Shane standing in the foyer holding another bouquet. This arrangement was of her actual favorite flower: orchids.

"Happy birthday, baby," he said, handing Philip the flowers and then cradling her face with both hands as he leaned down and kissed her softly.

"Thank you," she murmured against his lips.

"Welcome," he whispered before deepening the kiss. Wrapping his long arms around her waist, he pulled her body to his, moaning when her firm breasts pressed against his chest. The longing that he felt for her was evident in the way he panted shallow breaths, and his fingers dug into her hips. That familiar feeling, the bond they couldn't shake, swirled around them like a web.

"Ahem."

Clearing his throat, Philip snapped them out of their passion-induced haze.

"You can leave the flowers there," Shane said, pointing to a decorative table against the wall next to them. "That will be all for the night. Thanks, Phil."

Philip nodded. "Again, happy birthday, Ms. Joey."

"Thank you," Joey smiled, slightly embarrassed at losing herself so quickly. All of her best intentions went right out the window whenever Shane entered her orbit.

Once the door was closed, she looked up at him.

"Are we alone?"

"Yeah. I gave Allen and Estelle the weekend off."

"I'm sure we'll be able to fend for ourselves," she smirked.

"I think we'll be alright after the private chef leaves." He grinned, gesturing to her with his outstretched hand.

She placed her hand in his grasp and followed him until they walked out to the grotto. A small table was set with fancy silverware, crystal glassware, and a matching bucket with a bottle of champagne on ice. The area was dimly lit, with candlelight surrounding them, creating a romantic hue. Shane pulled out Joey's chair before sitting across from her. He made a show of popping the bottle before pouring them each a glass. He raised his drink to her.

"To my favorite person," he said before clinking her glass.

"That's the best you could come up with?" She teased.

"Well, I was going to ask how it felt to be old as hell but figured that might be rude.

"We're the same age, loser," she laughed.

"Technically, you're my elder. I don't turn twenty-seven until September.

"Kiss my ass!"

"No dessert before dinner, Joey!"

"Oh, shut up," she cackled. "You get on my damn nerves!"

"You love it." He waggled his brows, tipping her glass again as they finally drank to his toast.

"So, what happened? I thought we were meeting in Phoenix tomorrow?"

Shane's smile dimmed a bit, and he shrugged. "For one, I figured you'd enjoy this better."

"You're not wrong," she said, taking another sip.

"Two, Kelly's been in Phoenix all week. The WAGs had an event, so you know she had to show her face."

Joey rolled her eyes. "Of course."

Shane tilted his head to the side, assessing her tone.

"Don't act like that," he chided.

"Can we get through my birthday without mentioning her?"

"I was just being honest," he replied.

Joey released her aggravation in a sigh. "I know."

"It won't be much longer, Joey."

"Are you still coming to my opening this weekend?" She changed the subject, not wanting to bring the mood down anymore. She was opening up a dance studio for young dancers, something she had been working on for a while. Jackson and Shane were investors, and Joey was the owner/creative director. The studio would be used to hold classes and rented out for events.

"It's your birthday, so I won't say that was a stupid question. I'll just say yes. I'll be there."

Joey smirked. "Thanks, bestie."

"You're getting crotchety in your old age," he joked.

"You know what," she threatened to throw her drink on him, and he put his hands up in surrender.

"Ok! Ok! I'm sorry. Damn. I'm just tryin' to have a quiet dinner with my best friend. Is that so wrong?"

Joey swallowed her witty comeback with another sip of champagne and chuckled. She knew that if she let it, they'd be going back and forth all night. She also knew that all the tension between them had very little to do with them and everything to do with Kelly and Dante. She just didn't want to spend their night beating the same dead horse.

After dinner, they grabbed another bottle of bubbly and took a stroll down to the beach. Joey shared her excitement about the studio and working with young girls, and he filled her in on his plans to start a mentorship program with Jackson and Jay.

They usually spoke on a regular basis, but Joey had been avoiding him while she tried to work out her feelings. Relationships had been on the back burner for her until she reached a specific goal for her career. Now, she had no excuse, and two men were vying for her love.

"Why you so quiet?" Shane's question broke through her thoughts.

Joey was about to answer *nothing*, but that was a lie, and Shane would know it. She gazed at him momentarily before staring down at her toes as she dug them into the sand.

"I'm just wondering how this all plays out."

"So far, everything has gone the way you planned it. How do you want it to play out?"

Shane grabbed her hand and looked into her eyes. They'd both come a long way, with her tailored Saint Laurent utility dress and his Tom Ford suit. Her thighs were thicker than ever, and she had just the slightest pudge to her midsection that he loved even though she complained about being out of shape.

He didn't think there would ever be a version of Joey that he didn't love, adore, or need desperately.

"I'm working it all out," she said quietly.

"You need to decide what you want, Joey."

She nodded, staring out at the dark, crashing waves.

"I'll talk to Dante when he gets back. Just give me time. Your contract is almost up. There's no need to rush."

Shane's brows raised. "Are you saying what I think?"

"I'm saying, let's take things slow."

"I think I can live with that," he said, cupping her the back of the neck.

"You sure? 'cause you been calling me all hours of the day and night, even when you know I'm with Dante."

"Man, fuck Dante," he spat.

"Just let me handle things my way."

"Just hurry that shit up."

Joey shook her head as he brought his forehead to hers.

"I just need you to understand that you're mine. You're the only one here," he said, placing her hand over his heart. "This is forever for me. You got that?"

Joey shuddered at his words and trembled when he pressed his lips to hers. She was terrified of the future but even more terrified of a future without him in her life.

Chapter 5

"I now pronounce you man and wife," the minister said as the happy couple shared a lingering look of pure love and adoration. Remy smiled down at Chelle like she was his whole world. Towering over her despite her four-inch heels, he gently cradled her face in his large palms as he sealed their commitment with a kiss. It was a poignant moment, witnessing two of her closest friends tie the knot.

Joey clutched her bouquet tighter as she tried to calm her emotions and glanced at Nicole. They shared a teary-eyed smile as the couple's kiss went on and on, a testament to all they finally overcame to be together. Chelle was Joey's absolute best girlfriend in the world, and she was overjoyed to not only see her so happy but to see her happy with the love of her life.

It gave Joey hope that she might someday experience that kind of love. She tried to will her eyes not to wander, but she couldn't help but spare a peek at Shane. He was standing as one of Remy's groomsmen, and the smile he had on his face, warmed her heart. He was her best guy friend and probably knew more about her than Chelle did.

Over the years, Joey tried to reconcile her love for Shane because it ran so deep. So did her attraction to him, but they'd never been on the same page regarding being in a relationship. When he wanted her, she wasn't ready, and when she wanted him, he claimed she wasn't his type. After they graduated college, they maintained their friendship, and she was also his publicist, but their initial bond only deepened with time, not faded.

Then, she'd met Dante at Kiko's wedding three years prior, and they fit together well. However, they agreed to an open relationship due to their hectic work schedules. Joey didn't know if Dante was still exercising his option to see other people because if he did, he was very discreet about it, but she had suggested it more for the breathing room it gave her.

Throughout college, Joey was known for being a free spirit. Free to date whomever, whenever. Unlike her friend Nicole who'd been married since freshman year, and her other friend Kiko, who'd been with her boo Dom almost as long, Joey wasn't trying to settle down back then. She focused on her education and her goal of breaking into the world of Corporate America.

That's another reason she and Shane had maintained a friends with occasional benefits status. She didn't want a relationship, and his dream of being in the NBA was his priority. They both agreed that being exclusive wasn't in the cards and understood and supported each other in their goals. Jealousy and possessiveness had no room in their partnership.

They helped each other pick the right classes, with homework, projects and essays, and plan their futures. Sometimes, they even gave each other relationship advice. The biggest draw was that they had each other's backs during difficult times with their families.

Joey's grandmother had passed away in her freshman year, and Shane was there for her like he'd known her his entire life. Then, when he had drama with his family, she was able to help him sort through it. Those moments went a long way toward solidifying their connection.

Just looking at him, seeing his smile, and being near him during such an emotional moment made Joey want to run into his arms.

Freshman Year - 2003

True to his word, Shane helped Joey organize her travel back to Louisiana and helped with her grandmother's funeral. He and Jay helped her pack, from picking out what she needed based on the weather to ensuring she had the necessary toiletries. Then they returned to the dorms so Shane could pack his bag. He insisted they fly out that night and paid for the tickets even though she protested. It was then that she learned that his father, like hers, was very wealthy. Also, like her, Shane didn't have the best relationship with his parental unit.

The flight to New Orleans was quick, and in no time, they were exiting a taxi in front of the rustic 4th Ward home. Joey felt like time slowed down as she focused on everything but entering her childhood home. She watched Shane corral their bags, looked up and down the street at the neighboring houses and took her time fishing around for her key. Finally, Shane placed a reassuring hand on her back, following her up the path to the front door.

Taking a deep breath, Joey thrust the first key into the lock and then the key for the deadbolt. The familiar scent of home washed over her when she pushed the door open. The only thing missing was the aroma of a freshly cooked dinner or baked treat. Her grandmother was notorious for baking, and the kids in the neighborhood would always stop by for a cookie or sweet bread from Grann. Joey could always expect a delicious meal whenever she came home. Instead, it was stuffy with a slight trace of her grandmother's floral perfume.

Joey glanced around, noting a half-empty glass of sweet tea on the end table next to the sofa, the remote under the coffee table, and the back support cushion slightly askew. Taking it all in, she deduced that Grann must have been sitting down for her evening shows, as she called it, when she passed. The thought of it, and that she still wasn't sure of exactly what happened, brought the tears back to her eyes. She kept wishing she could hear Grann bustling in the kitchen or shuffling down the stairs.

Overcome with grief, she crumpled onto the couch, covering her face as she began to bawl. She almost forgot that Shane was with her until he sat beside her and wrapped an arm around her. He didn't speak, just sat there with her as she cried, and she was grateful. There wasn't anything that anyone could say that would help her feel any better. She was just glad not to have to face things alone.

After that, she was able to pull herself together enough to show Shane around the house. She helped him settle into the guest room before heading to her room. Other than pointing at the door, she didn't even attempt to enter her grandmother's room. A serial killer could have been waiting to off her, and she wouldn't have had a clue. She knew she'd have to deal with it eventually but wasn't ready.

She showered and changed for bed, creeping back down to the kitchen out of curiosity. Just as she suspected, there was a loaf of bread that was no more than a day old, a container with butterscotch chip cookies, and another container of brownies. Opening the fridge, she found it almost fully stocked and poured herself a glass of milk to go with a helping of everything she found. Sitting on the floor next to the couch, where she usually would as her grandmother played in her hair, she devoured her snacks. When she heard Shane coming down the stairs, she felt guilty for not inviting him to join her. She pretended she didn't know he was approaching her until his long legs were directly in front of her.

"I feel kinda betrayed." His smooth voice cut through the silence of the room.

"In my defense, I didn't want to wake you," she said, handing him a cookie as a peace offering.

"What's all this?"

"My grandmother was a baker, and I figured there would most likely be snacks in the kitchen."

"I don't know what kind of cookie this is, but it's changing my damn life," he said around a big bite.

"It's butterscotch chips. I refused to eat regular chocolate chips after she made them for the first time. There are also fudge brownies, sweet bread, and a homemade loaf of bread if you want."

"I want *alladat*!" He did a silly dance while pointing toward the kitchen, his Southern accent jumping out heavily.

After hooking Shane up with his own plate of treats, they sat and ate together. He asked Joey questions about her grandmother and her childhood, and she filled him in on her relationship with her mother, and the nonexistent relationship with her father. Shane's aunt, Tori, called him back while they talked, and he explained the situation to her. She said she could be there in two days and gave them instructions on who they needed to contact and what arrangements to make. She told Joey she would help her deal with the insurance company when she arrived.

Everything happened in a blur after that. The next day, she followed the list that Shane's aunt had given them, contacting the coroner and the funeral home. Joey was able to locate the insurance policy, which was locked in a safe with all of her grandmother's important documents. Shane went with her to claim the body, and the desolate expression in her eyes afterward gave him chills. He requested she show him around the city since they were so close to the French Quarter, and they hung out for the remainder of the day until she was so tired she barely had the energy to shower before she passed out.

When Tori arrived, she gave Joey a big hug and expressed her condolences. Joey admired Shane's relationship with his aunt, who he claimed he was closer to than his mother. He also shared a bit about his strained relationship with his parents, but where Joey had to fend for herself, his parents spoiled him to make up for the fact that they were never around.

The call to the insurance company had been enlightening because Joey learned that not only was she the sole beneficiary of the policy, but the amount had been increased to two hundred and fifty thousand dollars a few years prior. She literally clutched her chest when she heard that number and realized that there was an entirely different policy to pay for the funeral costs.

"If I were you, I would keep that information to myself," Tori advised after Joey hung up the call.

"Is it terrible that I was already thinking that? My mother was already giving me a song and dance about the cost of plane tickets and not being able to come to the damn funeral."

"It seems like you've had a rough go of it, but your grandmother had your back," Tori replied.

Tori and Shane were with Joey every step of the way, from the funeral arrangements to the guest list, flowers, food, and even contacting an estate lawyer about the house. Joey was torn between keeping or selling the house, but Tori urged her not to decide while she was still emotionally raw. In the meantime, she hired a property manager to deal with renters and the house's upkeep.

The funeral itself was beautiful. Her grandmother had left detailed instructions of how she wanted her sendoff to be. All her friends from church, the neighborhood, and a few friends from her old job were in attendance. A few of Joey's distant relatives were able to make it, and to her surprise, her mother *and* her father showed up. The love for Grann was very evident and gave Joey a sense of comfort.

Of course, the first thing her mother asked about was how she paid for the funeral, and what the insurance policy looked like. True to the plan, Joey showed her the death benefit payment that barely covered the cost of the funeral and told her she had no plans of selling the house. Of course, the questions came, and the will proved that her grandmother did, in fact, leave the house to Joey.

Her father's presence was a total surprise. Apparently, he kept up with Joey via her grandmother. He said he had to pay his respects to the woman who raised his daughter. Joey could have sworn she sensed an air of regret emanating from him, but she didn't explore whether that was true or not.

A wealthy music mogul, her father had never been a significant part of her life. He sent money to her grandmother for her care, but his physical presence was glaringly absent. He would call every so often to inquire about her schooling and question her goals. He'd funded her dance activities and had some weird obsession with her becoming a ballerina.

When she stated her goals as a businesswoman, he expressed his displeasure and refused to help her with her degree unless she changed her mind and acquiesced to his request. Stubborn as a bull, Joey refused and declared she'd figure it out on her own. Even her mother had tried to convince her to accept his offer, explaining that if she cooperated, she would have it made because he would fund her college experience, but Joey wasn't having it.

As usual, he expressed his disappointment in her not pursuing dance but seemed to warm up to her career plans. His trip was quick, in and out in one day, but Joey appreciated the effort, even if she felt even more disconnected from her parents than usual. Neither one of them did much by way of consoling her or helping her to find her footing, so she was eternally grateful for Shane and Tori.

When it was all said and done, and they were back in Florida, Joey felt a sense of relief. Of course, the sadness from her grandmother was still there and would always be there, but the support she received from Shane was life-affirming. She watched him as he drove them out of the airport, having left his car in long-term parking so they didn't have to worry about transportation when they landed, and wondered what she would have done if she had listened to her brain and not befriended him.

"Thank you for everything," she said, giving his arm an affectionate squeeze.

"I got you," he replied with a smile. "I'm just glad I drove by when I did that day. It scares me to think about what would have happened if I hadn't."

"I don't even really remember anything before you put me in your car," she sighed. "I'm scared to think about what would have happened to me, too."

"Well, luckily, we don't have to."

Shane pulled into the parking lot of the Townsend Efficiencies but didn't cut his engine.

"I guess this is my stop," Joey said with fake enthusiasm.

"I was thinking," Shane said while looking around. "I don't think it's a good idea for you to stay here. It's not that safe, and after seeing what happened the other day, you really should be on campus. Especially now that you can officially quit your job."

"I mean, I was thinking about that too, but I don't get my on-campus housing until next semester, and any place that will give me a short-term lease will look just like this." She shrugged.

"Why don't you stay on campus with me? I mean, I have a double room to myself, and no one will bother you. It's just for a few months."

He watched her with an expectant brow raised, waiting for her response. They stared at each other for a moment, curious about what the other was thinking. She was flat-out shocked at the offer but could totally consider it after the few days they'd spent together getting to know each other even better. He hoped she took his offer at face value and didn't think he was trying to be a creep. His aunt suggested the idea when he told her about the circumstances surrounding the day Joey received the bad news.

"Are you sure? I don't want you to get in trouble with the athletic department. The team can't afford to lose you."

"Trust me, Coach won't give me a problem; you're family. Ok?"

"Why are you doing all this? Being so nice and helping me like this?" Joey was genuinely baffled by all his kindness and helpfulness.

"Because I'm your friend," he simply replied.

"Ok." Joey agreed, with a smile. "I'll stay on campus with you, *friend*."

Shane gave her a high five before helping her pack what few belongings she did have into his car. Joey's mood was lighter than it had been since even before she found out about her grandmother, and she was actually, *finally*, excited about her college experience instead of feeling like an imposter. She watched Shane as he goofed off and danced around while moving her stuff, and she joined him, sending up a silent prayer and thank you to her grandmother.

Chapter 6

After a *dramatically* long kiss, Remy swept his bride into his arms and carried her down the aisle and out the church doors, garnering cheers from the crowd. Behind them, each couple in the wedding party followed. Joey linked arms with Jay after Kiko, the Matron of Honor, Remy's best friend Dom, who happened to be her husband, and Shane and Nicole. It was rare, but most of the couples in their little crew had been together since college. Even Chelle and Remy had been high school sweethearts who reconnected years later. That was why Joey and Shane kept some of the facets of their relationship under wraps. They didn't want the pressure from the other couples to determine their path.

Outside the church, the wedding party crowded together as the photographer snapped a few pictures. As usual, Shane was behind Joey, pressed against her back while they took silly candid photos until the newlyweds jumped into their limo to take their official pictures. The remaining bridal party, consisting of two of Chelle's cousins, loaded into their Mercedes Sprinter while the groomsmen entered theirs.

"I felt like I was gonna cry my damn eyes out," Kiko exclaimed once they were settled.

"Honestly," Joey agreed. "I still feel like crying. I'm so damn happy for Chelle and Remy!"

"I know!" Nicole said as she swiped at the ruined makeup under her eyes as she checked herself in a compact mirror. "Especially with everything they went through. Can you believe Kiko's wedding was already three years ago?"

Kiko shook her head ruefully. "It feels like yesterday and forever ago, all at the same time," she sighed. Joey glanced at her curiously, unsure if she was being whimsical or sarcastic.

"Is the honeymoon phase over?" Joey cocked an eyebrow.

Kiko chuckled. "I guess you could say that. Once baby comes, all bets are off."

"I can't wait to see my lil munchkins," Joey squealed, thinking about Kiko and Nicole's little ones.

Both Kiko and Nicole had babies, one year apart, who were at the church but wouldn't be part of the reception since it was for adults only. Chelle and Remy paid for professional childcare for those parents who wanted to check in on their kids during the celebration. It was being held at an upstate winery about an hour outside Manhattan. It was perfect weather for their favorite couple; the warm summer day was beautiful, with the sun shining brightly and not a cloud in the sky.

Once at the reception hall, the group mixed and mingled with the other guests and the couple's parents. Their mothers had become a friend group of their own over the years, with Remy's mother being the last on board. Nicole and Chelle's mothers had known each other since the girls were in high school, and then Jay's mother joined them during college.

The only mothers not in attendance were Joey's, who never really took an interest in her collegiate journey due to the demands of her gaggle of small children, and Shane's, who was practically living in Europe. For the most part, the extended family vibe worked, considering how close their children were and their shared plans for success. Joey is the publicist, Chelle is the lawyer, Remy is the sports agent, Kiko is a personal stylist, and Nicole is the journalist. Shane and Jay are NBA stars, and Kiko's husband, Dom, was a huge star in the NFL. They were a force to be reckoned with, for sure.

Once at the banquet hall, everyone snacked on hors d'oeuvres and sipped champagne during the fancy cocktail hour. There was a bit of tension as Joey tried her best to navigate being in the same room as Dante and Shane. He was there without his girlfriend, Kelly, but Dante had returned from his trip to Africa to attend the wedding with Joey. That had always been the plan.

Dante wasn't feeling her relationship with Shane, and the two men had been exchanging tense glances during the course of the day. Over the three years she'd been dating him, he'd grown increasingly weary of how close Joey and Shane were. His main complaint was that Joey seemed to spend more time on the phone with Shane than she did with him in real life. Since he also worked for the same company as Joey, he wasn't about to make a scene, but the negative vibes could be felt, nonetheless.

To his credit, Shane kept his distance with his physical presence, at least. His eyes were another story. He'd been staring Joey down during the exchange of vows. And even though he might be across the room, Joey kept meeting his intense gaze. She couldn't help it. It was torture to not be near him, but she had to get her shit sorted out with Dante. He'd just returned from a two-month trip to Africa to help the NFL start a mini-league, but they hadn't had a chance to talk about their future together or much of anything.

Knowing Shane how she did, he wouldn't be quiet for long and wouldn't let the day go without them talking.

"What's on your mind?" Dante handed her a glass of champagne while he surveyed the room.

"Oh, you know," she gestured around the venue. "Happy endings and all that. I almost bawled my eyes out during the ceremony."

"I noticed that," he said, catching her roaming eyes. "What's up with that?"

"What do you mean?"

"Well, you've been all anti-marriage since we met. At least that's what you told me. It's interesting to see you get so worked up."

"I'm not anti-marriage," she corrected. "I'm just not ready to settle down."

He smirked. "At all, or just with me?"

It was her turn to make a face. "Are you ready to settle down? *Mr. 'I don't do monogamy'.*"

"Oh, you got jokes," he chuckled at her imitating his voice.

"I mean," she laughed. "That was you, right?" She nudged his shoulder, and he slid his arm around her waist, kissing her ear. Joey tried her best not to tense up because she just knew that Shane was somewhere watching, and even though, technically, she wasn't doing anything wrong, she still felt guilty as hell. Something had to give because she felt like her carefully arranged house of cards was about to be demolished.

"I've thought about it," Dante admitted. "As much as I love what we have going, I do want a family." He pinned her with a sober gaze as he waited for her response.

Joey's chest ached because this was her worst fear. She'd dragged her feet in deciding to end things with Dante, and now he suggested taking things to the next level. It wasn't that she didn't have feelings for him because she did. She loved Dante and often wondered what he would be like as a husband and father. On paper, he was everything that she said she was looking for, but her feelings for him just didn't go deep enough.

"Well, I'm not having kids in an open relationship," she replied flatly.

"So, let's close it."

Joey gave him a skeptical glare.

"Just like that?"

"I don't see what the issue is."

"There's no issue, but I'm just wondering where all this is even coming from."

"Well, I guess weddings have that effect on people. I met you at a wedding, and now here we are, three years later. I feel like we've come full circle."

Joey sipped on her champagne as he talked, glancing around the room, trying not to cut him off and tell him that she thought he was full of shit. He only wanted to close things up to trump Shane and try to change the narrative. He never came out and asked her if the relationship with Shane was sexual in nature, but Joey was beginning to think he'd be ok with that as long as there wasn't any emotional connection.

"I think this is a conversation to have when you get back from your trip," she suggested.

Dante was going on another two-month excursion to Africa, and that alone made the entire conversation ridiculous to her. Not only was he not in a place to settle down, familywise, but him being away so often meant that she would have to give up her career to be a stay-at-home mom, and if she was going to do that...

Joey glanced at Shane, standing with Jackson, Nicole and Jay. He pretended to listen as Jackson explained something with animated hand gestures, but his eyes wandered. Joey chuckled to herself, knowing he wasn't focused on that conversation at all. There was never a wrong time to talk business as far as Jackson was concerned. Shane's eyes flitted to her at that moment and crinkled with humor.
As usual, they were on the same page. She really looked at him for the first time that day, noticing how his body had bulked up a little and his tuxedo was fitting just right. His usually wild, curly fro was tamed with product and nicely defined. He'd cut down his goatee and beard and almost looked like he did back when they graduated college.

If I'm going to give up my life, it will be for him.

∞

"Girl," Nicole drawled. "What is this tension between you and Shane? I feel like it's giving *me* anxiety!"

"Yeah," Kiko chimed in. "And why does Dante seem like he's on the brink?"

Joey released a heavy sigh. "It's a long ass story."

"Would it have anything to do with your trip to Italy?" Nicole mumbled under her breath so that only Joey and Kiko could hear.

"That, among other things," Joey snorted. "Of course, it's the usual shit about how close I am with Shane."

Nicole smirked but didn't say a word. She and Joey had grown closer since her engagement and the birth of her child, and she was very well aware of just how close Joey and Shane *really* were. Especially since she hosted them when they coincidentally visited her and Jay in Italy at the same time. Nicole was aware that the duo never returned to the hotel on the night of Shane's birthday dinner. She accepted that it was up to Joey and Shane to make sense of what they had going on. Raising a baby and planning a wedding helped to curb her usual nosiness.

"Well, as long as they both continue to play nice on tuh-day, everything should be good," Kiko joked.

"Yeah, Dante is too logical to cause an issue. Trust me," Joey replied.

"I still don't get the dynamics of it all," Kiko sighed. "But if you like it, I love it."

Joey shrugged as the intro to "Reunited" by Peaches and Herb began to play. Everyone let out a collective chuckle at the couple referencing their breakup. The high school sweethearts had spent over eight years separated by an ugly rumor. Once they hashed it out, it became undeniable that time hadn't diminished an ounce of their love for each other.

"Everyone! Please clear the dance floor and give a huge welcome to Mr. and Mrs. *Spencer!*" The DJ repeated the song's chorus as the couple two-stepped their way to the middle of the dance floor. Once Remy spun Chelle into his arms, the song changed to a slow piano ballad as "I Believe In You And Me" by The Four Tops played.

"Ladies and gentlemen, Groom's choice," The DJ announced.

It was just like Chelle and Remy to have a medley of songs for their first dance. Music played an integral role during the early years of their relationship and was part of the glue that bonded their souls together. The deep baritone voice of the lead singer crooned to his lady love about how he believed in her and their love, and how they would be in love eternally. She would always be the one. It perfectly described Remy's feelings for Chelle, even during their time apart.

Joey felt the emotions swirling around inside her again. When the lyrics described love as a miracle, she felt the urge to sob and couldn't understand why she was so damn worked up. She kept her eyes focused on the beautiful couple, which didn't help because Chelle had tears trailing down her cheeks as she smiled up at Remy. It was such a tender moment; it almost felt wrong to watch them.

She could feel eyes on her, and when she glanced up, Shane was staring right at her. He was just as sensitive as her, deep down. The plan was for them both to end their current relationships, and he was there alone while she was there with Dante. She knew he wasn't happy about it, and would corner her at some point, but she wasn't ready to deal with it.

Then the song flowed into the angelic crooning of Mariah Carey as she recalled her "Vision of Love." Chelle's choice, as explained by DJ Randy B. Joey smiled as memories of Chelle playing that song on repeat in their dorm room flashed in her mind. She glanced at Nicole and Kiko, who both returned a knowing look. Even though she had kept many things to herself, deep down, Chelle always held a torch for Remy. Watching how he enveloped her in his arms as the song outlined her emotions from gratitude and love to despair and feeling alienated made Joey's heart flutter.

"Now it's time for the wedding party to join the couple on the dancefloor."

Jay reached for Joey's hand and led her onto the dance floor as the song transitioned into "Endless Love" by Luther Vandross and Mariah Carey, a duet of two lovers professing their undying love for each other. It was obviously a song picked by the couple or one of "their" songs because they both knew all the lyrics and sang the song to each other. When Chelle emoted the female lover's part, Remy, overcome with emotion, rested his forehead against hers. It was a touching sight to see him being so vulnerable.

As they danced, Jay kept adjusting their position so that he would always face Nicole, until he spun Joey into Shane's arms to exchange partners. Shane grinned down at her as he pulled her against his solid chest. Joey sighed and settled into his embrace, his strong arms wrapping around her and holding her close. He placed a quick kiss on her forehead, too overcome with emotion for her to hold back. Not caring who saw or what they thought or felt about it.

The tears came then. Joey couldn't hold back anymore. She had been sentimental at Kiko's wedding, it was her nature, but something about Chelle's wedding was breaking her all the way down. It could have been because it was her best friend, the circumstances that the couple had to overcome, or the fact that she'd been having more and more visions of her own happy ending. More than ever before, she could picture herself as not only a wife but a mother, too, especially after spending so much time with Nicole's little one.

Shane just held her to his chest while she struggled to compose herself. The fact that she'd missed him so much, how safe she felt in his arms, and that Dante was somewhere watching were all eating her up. She knew that she couldn't put off deciding any longer. Her heart called for her to take a chance with Shane, but he hadn't cleaned up his life to be ready for her either.

An irrational need for more was replacing all the logical reasons she had for not wanting a serious relationship. She didn't know when it started, but it was happening. Sometimes, she daydreamed about her own babies, making a home, and being loved by an adoring husband. Shane made her heart flutter, but Dante was more stable and gave her the space she needed.

In Italy, Shane had flat-out vowed that he would, that he could, be the man that she needed. He promised to convince her that they were meant for each other and that their love was more profound than a friends with benefits situation. And she wanted to believe him and believe that everything he had said was true, but his erratic behavior on and off the basketball court made her nervous.

The problem wasn't that Joey didn't trust him to be a man of his word, she was afraid of things not working and them losing their friendship. Sure, they were already close, so why not just take that next step? But he had been so adamant that she wasn't the type of woman he wanted for the mother of his children, which hurt, and she wasn't jumping to test out his epiphany.

"What's wrong?" Shane's lower register tickled her ear, and she shrugged.

"I don't know," she sighed. "I just feel hella emotional."

"You missed me," he said as if he was confident that was the problem.

"That might be part of it."

"I hate being away from you," he murmured. "I hate knowing you're with him when I'm thinking about you. I hate that you're not with me every night."

"Shane," she whimpered.

"You got me out here feeling crazy," he went on. "Like right now, all I can think about is kidnapping your ass and taking you back to Italy."

Joey smiled despite her tears. "That was fun."

"It was," he agreed. "But it's always that way with us. Right? It's always you for me. I'm sorry that I ever said anything different."

He held her tighter after that admission, and a shudder of unbridled emotion coursed through her as she attempted to stop crying. The song's lyrics intertwining with Shane's confession wasn't helping her to calm down.

"I got you," he promised against her ear.

Joey just nodded as her fingers dug into him tighter. In that moment, she felt like she never wanted to let him go. Every reason they had not to be together seemed silly because it felt so right to be in his arms. She clung to him like a lifeline, letting her heart and soul bask in their connection.

He stroked her arm soothingly with one hand while the other was planted firmly against her back, keeping her pressed to him. Neither of them noticed that the song had changed and that the DJ had called for everyone to join the couple on the dance floor. They were in their own cocoon of love.

Until Dante tapped Shane on the shoulder.

Chapter 7

"May I cut in?" Dante had asked a question, but the expression in his eyes, coupled with the fact that he was already attempting to extract Joey from Shane's embrace, exposed it for the demand that it was.

"Not yet," Shane replied. Looking down on Dante like he was inconsequential.

"Joey." Dante's tone was terse and gritty. His hand at her elbow slid up to her wrist as he moved to slip his hand in hers to pull her away.

"*Nigga*," Shane growled. "I said not yet. Step off."

Shane shoved Dante's arm away, which caused the other man to square up as a reflex. Even though Shane was taller, they were both athletes. Dante was an ex-football player, and not only would an altercation between them not end well, but it would ruin her friend's day.

"Hey, why don't we all just take a moment," Dom said, stepping in and placing one hand on Shane's back and the other on Dante's shoulder, closing the group in and containing the mounting drama.

"Look, Shane," Dante said. "I don't want any problems with you."

"So then back the fuck up," Shane replied. "I'm talking to my friend. She'll come to you when she's ready."

Dom looked between the three of them, and the fact that Joey had tears in her eyes but was still clinging to Shane told him what he needed to do. "Come on, Dante," he said as he guided him away. "Give her a little space. You know how weddings do some people."

Furious, Dante looked deep into Joey's eyes, shrugged off Dom's hold and walked away calmly, exiting out the side door of the venue. Dom shook his head, glancing at Joey and Shane curiously before bumping fists with Shane and returning to his wife.

Dante's intrusion had burst their little bubble, and Joey swiped at her eyes and straightened her back.

"I should go talk to him."
"If that mutha-fucka acts up again, I'm gonna rock his shit," Shane threatened.
"He didn't act up. He was just trying to dance with his girlfriend," she pointed out.
"You need to end that shit."
"As soon as you end things with Kelly," she tossed back.
"Are you being serious? She's not here, is she? Do I lay up with her every night?"
"This isn't the time or the place for this," she snarled through her teeth. "And we've

talked it into the ground. You know where I stand. Now, please. I need to go talk to Dante. After this, *he's* probably gonna break up with *me*."

"I hope and pray," Shane muttered as he turned to walk away, shoving his hands in the pockets of his trousers.

Shaking her head at his sarcasm, Joey took a deep breath to compose herself. She glanced around, catching both Nicole and Kiko glaring at her, and knew she was going to catch hell for that little spat. Snagging a cloth napkin from her place setting to dab at her eyes, she headed for the exit that Dante left out of.

It didn't take long for her to find him, staring out at the pond behind the venue. His palms were placed flat against the wooden banister as he leaned forward. Joey strolled up behind him and placed a hand on his back. He didn't turn to face her but glanced down over his shoulder at her. When she didn't say anything, he looked away.

"What's going on, Joey? Why does it feel like I'm your side dude?"

"Dante, you know you're not my side dude."

"Does Shane know that?" He turned to face her then. "What does he know that has him acting like you're his woman and not mine?"

"You know he's just protective of me. He–"

"Just stop. I don't want to hear that lame ass excuse anymore. None of my friends or exes act like this. Does anyone in my life disrespect you?"

She heaved a sigh. "No."

"Joey," he said, placing his fingertip to her chin and caressing her jaw. "I love you, but I can't play this game anymore. We can either be exclusive, or we can end it. I'm not coming in second anymore. You can give me your decision when I come back from Ghana."

He kissed her lightly on the forehead and then her lips, but the thud of footsteps approaching interrupted their moment.

"Shane? What are you doing?" Joey asked, noticing the fire in his eyes and the aggressive way he was charging toward Dante.

"I think we need to get a few things straight," Dante said preemptively, stepping away from Joey and into Shane's path.

"Nah, I think you're the only one that needs to get shit straight," Shane grunted as he came to a stop in front of the other man.

"*I* need to get shit straight? You –"

"You need to learn your fuckin' place. I'm tired of your corny ass interrupting and buttin' into our business every time I'm talking to her."

"Joey *is* my damn business," Dante shouted.

"That's where you're wrong," Shane retorted. "She's *my* fuckin' business, and it's about time you accept that shit."

Shane stepped closer, forcing Dante to look up at him.

"Back the fuck up, Duncan," Dante warned, his fists balled at his sides. Joey finally snapped out of her shock and tried to break things up.

"Hold on," she huffed, pushing at both of their chests. "I'm my own damn business. What the fuck?"

"I think we all know what it is." Shane's head tilted to the side as he regarded Dante. "Why you think you can't have her all to yourself and have to settle for an open relationship?"

"You're the one settling for my sloppy seconds," Dante taunted, shoving Shane in the chest. Shane simply laughed before grabbing the shoulder of Dante's suit and hitting him with a quick jab to the face.

"Shane, no!" Joey whisper-screamed, grabbing his arm as he pulled back to hit Dante again. At the same moment, Jay and Dom came trotting up to them to break up the scuffle. There were a few tense moments of grunting and growls as Dante attempted to hit Shane back, but Shane clocked him in the side of the head while the other men struggled to pull them apart.

"Come on, man," Jay said as he firmly pulled Shane away by his midsection.

"Y'all can't be serious," Dom hissed.

"This is what I'm talking about, Joey," Dante tossed over Dom's shoulder. "I'm not putting up with this shit!" He shrugged out of Dom's hold and stormed off, again.

"That's right! Walk the fuck away, *bitch*," Shane shouted over Jay's arm.

"Will you chill the fuck out," Jay chided as he guided his friend away.

"Joey? You good?"

Joey nodded, vaguely hearing Dom's question as she stood there stunned, staring as Dante's retreating form drifted further and further away.

"Hey," Nicole's raspy voice floated over her shoulder. Joey had been so deep in thought that she hadn't even heard her come out. "What was that all about?"

"Please," Joey sighed. "I can't take a lecture right now."

"Girl, please," Nicole said, slipping an arm around Joey's shoulder. "I just came to make sure you're ok. I'm filling in for Chelle since she can't be on mama bear duty today."

Joey chuckled. "Thank you."

"Come inside. It's almost time to eat, and then we have the toasts. By then, you'll be ready to have some fun. Wait, where's Dante going?"

"He's leaving," Joey replied with a befuddled expression.

"I'm sorry, boobie," Nicole crooned. "That's what Chelle would say, right?"

"It's bookie," Joey smirked. "And she would give me a hug and a little pep talk."

"I got you on the hug; you gonna have to pretend on the rest," Nicole joked. She threw both arms around Joey and held her close. "I wish you and Shane would quit your shit and work this out. I know I was in denial about Jay, but you and Shane have been doing this shit for too damn long, and it's getting messy. End it before it gets any worse.

Joey nodded. "I know."

"But for now..." Nicole grabbed her hand and led her back toward the reception. "Let's go finish celebrating our girl."

∞

Things calmed back down after the incident, and the rest of the reception went off without a hitch. Remy and Chelle had planned a fun night for their guests with lots of dancing and trivia games to get everyone involved. Joey tried her best to put the fight behind her and enjoy the party, finding it easier to go with that flow after Dante left. She realized that part of her stress was that she knew she needed to end things with him because his insecurity was driving him to be more possessive. She felt stifled.

On the other hand, Shane's possessiveness made her feel all warm and fuzzy inside, even if he was acting like a psycho.

"My Boo" by Usher and Alicia Keys played, and she swayed to the music as she sipped a glass of champagne.

"My Boo," Chelle crooned in her ear as she wrapped her arms around Joey.

"I love you," Joey sighed as she hugged Chelle back.

"I love you more, bookie. That's why I'm not gonna kick your ass for trying to turn my wedding into a WWE live event!"

"Chelle! I swear that shit just unfolded right before my eyes," Joey cried.

"I know," Chelle giggled. "I saw the way Shane stormed outta here. Remy and I may or may not have tangoed toward the window to see what was going down."

"Seriously?" Joey pulled back to look Chelle in the face.

"I don't know what Dante said, but I know Shane deaded it."

"Chelle," Joey gasped. "Stop it! That was so crazy. Why is your boy acting a fool?"

"You know why," Chelle retorted with a sly glance. "Got his pretty face scratched up in the process."

Joey pouted. "Thank God, it isn't too bad."

"But seriously, babe. Fix it. That's what you do for everyone else, right?"

"I will."

"I know you will." Chelle squeezed her tight as Bobby Valentino's "Slow Down" began to play. It was one of the girls' favorite songs from college.

"Slow down!" They both sang the words as Kiko and Nicole joined them. They all danced around Chelle, who did her signature shoulder shimmy. Soon, Remy joined her in the crew's center as the guys joined them before they all broke off to dance with their respective partners. Shane and Joey were left dancing near each other when he stretched out his hand for her to dance.

"You mad at me, Juicy?"

"I should be," she said as she took his hand, accepting his offer.

"I'm sorry," he said before spinning her into his arms.

She didn't respond right away. She was a little upset, even if Chelle wasn't. How could he risk ruining the day over something so silly? But being near him and enveloped by his presence caused the slow familiar heat to rise up her spine.

"You should be," she said finally. "I don't understand what that was all about?"

"You don't?"

She shook her head, looking around to see who was watching. Everyone was. Not wanting to cause another scene, she let him continue to spin her around until they were no longer the center of attention. Then attempted to wiggle out of his grasp.

"Where are you going?" He asked with an incredulous stare.

"To get some fresh air," she replied.

Her thoughts were going a mile a minute and her emotions weren't far behind. Grabbing another glass of champagne, she headed back outside and toward the pond. There was an official terrace where guests could congregate and take pictures, but she wanted to be by herself. She was outside for about thirty seconds before Shane came following her out.

"Agh," she growled, eyes to the sky. "Can I get some time to think?"

"Cut it out," he said as he leaned against the railing beside her. "I didn't even say anything to you."

"You don't have to, Shane. I know you. I know what's on your mind and I know what you want. I know your damn thoughts!"

"Damn," he said with a raised brow and hands. "I wasn't trying to impose."

"Yes you were," she retorted. "Your presence is imposing. You just standing here makes me –"

"Makes you what?" He asked, crowding her like she accused him of, and twirling a few loose strands of her hair around his finger.

"Nothing," she huffed, not wanting to say out loud how he made her feel.

"Why'd you stop? Makes you what? Feel loved? Happy?"

She sighed, refocusing her attention on the pond. It was dark, and the moon's reflection rippled across the surface.

"Is that why you've been avoiding me? You don't want to admit how much we fit? How right it feels when we're together."

"Dante said he wants to be exclusive."

Shane didn't reply, just glared at her to continue.

"I mean I'm sure it's over after what happened earlier. Why did you do it?"

"Because, you're mine and I'm tired of acting like you're not."

"I had a plan, Shane. Why couldn't you just let me do it my way."

Shane placed his hands on her shoulders and turned her to face him. He peered into her eyes, trying to get to her, to get her to see what they had and quit running from it.

"It made me crazy to see him touch you. I don't care who the fuck he's supposed to be. You promised me this is what you wanted. If you don't want it anymore, tell me. Tell me so I can start over and show you why we belong together again."

"Shane," she sighed as her heart swooned.

"Tell me you don't love me anymore, Joey. Go ahead."

"You know I can't say that."

"Then tell me you love me and kiss me like you've missed me as much as I missed you."

It was useless to refuse him. Joey reached up on her tiptoes, using her fingertips to trace his eyebrows as he leaned into her touch.

"I love you," she whispered against his lips.

"And?" He brushed his lips against hers.

"I missed you. So damn much."

Shane pulled her against him and pressed his mouth to hers, slicing his tongue past her lips. She moaned as she finally succumbed to what she realized was longing for him. All day her body had been craving his touch and to be in his arms, but she felt conflicted because of Dante. With him being gone, there was nothing holding her back, so she gave in to the feeling.

Her soft whimpers grew into tortured moans as his hands began to roam the curves of her body. The off-shoulder bridesmaid dress offered enough exposed skin for him to kiss and caress.

"Are we good? I don't want to go through this again. I'm starting to feel like I'm going a little crazy," Shane admitted. His hips grinding against her as the bulge in his pants hit critical mass.

"We're good," Joey sighed as his fingers tweaked and pinched her nipple through the smooth satin bodice of her dress, causing her to strain against him. Her breathing became shallow as the need in her body increased.

"Shane," she gasped when his teeth pierced the tender flesh of her ear lobe.

He swept her up in his arms in a flash, looking around for a more private spot. Joey didn't even bother asking him what he was doing because this is what they always did. They ignored their desire for each other for too long, and then combusted whenever they came near to each other. It was a heady cycle that neither of them could seem to break.

"Shane," she moaned deeply when his hand slipped underneath the slit of her dress and traveled up her thigh. His middle finger teased her slit as his thumb pressed against the bundle of nerves that was straining through her panties. "Please," she begged.

"Please, stop or please, keep going?" His voice rumbled against her ear.

"We've gotta get back inside," she groaned. "Before someone comes looking for us."

"Then I guess we better hurry," he grunted.

"You're so crazy," she whispered, but didn't make any attempt to stop him when he turned her to face the brick wall.

The thud of the bass from the music inside was vibrating off the windows, and Joey could hear the crowd singing along to "Let Me Hold You" by Bow Wow and Omarion. She doubted anyone was worried about them. A shiver rippled through her and the searing heat of anticipation singed her from the inside out when she heard the clink of his belt buckle as he undid his pants. One hand was back under her dress strumming her clit like a guitar and she rolled her hips trying to find her rhythm.

"Bend forward."

He urged her to arch her back and angled her body toward him. Sliding her thong to the side, he wasted no time sliding inside her until he was so deep she whimpered his name. Then he pulled back slowly, repeating that motion a few times before he began to speed up his strokes.

"Oh, shit," she moaned, biting her lip to keep from getting too loud.
"Shit, you're so fucking wet," he groaned.
"Uh! Just like that," she gritted between her teeth. "Don't you fuckin' stop!"
"Uh hmm. You like that deep stroke. Keep taking all that dick."

Shane slipped both arms around her waist, lifting her off the ground so he could pull her back as he pushed deep inside her. He began to pump into her rougher and wilder until he was practically growling with each stroke. Joey's hands flailed forward, using the wall to brace herself as her climax surged from her core. She gasped with every thrust, bucking her hips to match his frenetic pace.

"Ahh, yes," she hissed as her orgasm broke.

"Yeah, baby," he groaned over and over until he was jerking as he reached his own peak. His knees wobbled, and he spun around to use the wall for support. He held her back to his chest while he placed a path of soft kisses from her neck to her ear. "Actin' like you didn't miss me," he huffed.

"Shut up," Joey laughed as she fought to get her breathing under control.

They were both silent as they came down from their high, and clarity set in. Joey fixed her hair and dress, making sure there weren't any tell-tale signs of what they'd just done. Shane tucked himself back in and straightened his suit. Then they checked each other to make sure they covered all bases. Like quality control. It was like a ritual to them.

"You know," he said as he smoothed down her side swoop bang. "As fun as these little clandestine meetings are, I'm tired of us being a secret."

"I know," she sighed. "And I promise we won't have to do this for much longer."

"You've been saying that for years now, Joey. I'm patient, and I understand that the timing was off for both of us, but I'm at a point in my life where I really don't give a fuck what anyone thinks. And I know you're gonna say that's counterproductive to my career, but I just don't care. The money don't mean shit without you."

He caressed her cheek with his thumb as he peered into her eyes with a look that she felt in the depths of her soul. There was no point in trying to argue or disagree because she knew he was right. The altercation with Dante was the final straw. She knew that. Neither man would be ok going back to how it was.

"After your trade goes through and you officially break up with Kelly, we'll be free and clear. Stop acting like you don't have to get your shit straight."

"I know what I have to do, but like I said. I'm over hiding. I'm prepared to deal with the fallout. We wouldn't be the first couple to cause a scandal, and we won't be the last."

"That's easy for you to say. Your career can take the hit. I literally get paid to prevent situations like this."

"Joey? Do you know I'm a multi-millionaire? You can quit your fucking job and do just about anything you want. There's no excuse. Not a good one, at least."

"It's not just a job, Shane. It's what I love to do. It's what I want to do. So, we're going to do this the right way."

He shook his head and shrugged in defeat. "It's your call, boss."

Chapter 8

"Chelle and Remy's wedding was just what I expected," Kiko said as she sipped a peach Bellini.

The girls, minus Chelle who was on her honeymoon in Bali, were on a girl's trip to Catalina Island. Joey said it was to celebrate the honeymoon in their own way, but the truth was, she just really missed her friends. She was the only one living on the west coast and didn't get to see the others as often, but all that was about to change. They all had to fly back to Cali for various reasons, Nicole because Jay had tryouts with a couple of the L.A. teams, Kiko because Dom had a preseason scrimmage, and of course Joey lived out there. It was rare for them all to be in the same place, so they took advantage of it.

They were having lunch at a bistro overlooking the sparkling blue harbor after taking a helicopter tour of the island.

"It was almost as perfect as I expected," Nicole said, with a serious side-eye to Joey.

"Ok, now y'all gotta fill me in on what I missed. Dom wouldn't let me come outside when everything was going down, but I did see Shane kinda handle Dante on the dancefloor."

"Must we?" Joey sighed.

"Don't look at me," Nicole said and then sipped her drink. "I'm in the business of minding my business these days."

"Well, I don't care who tells the story as long as it gets told," Kiko replied, rolling her eyes.

Joey hesitated, not sure where to start. Should she just recap the wedding or jump back to Italy or their college days? Kiko didn't know about that part, and it was kind of important to explain just why Shane was acting batshit crazy. Just thinking about it, she realized how long she and Shane had been nursing their feelings for each other.

"Ok." She cleared her throat as she began. "When we were in Italy, Shane said he wanted us to be together."

"No!" Nicole's fake gasp startled Kiko, who was leaning in for the tea and let a little yelp, almost knocking over her drink. The other girls cracked up at her theatrics.

"Seriously," Joey cried.

"Wait. I feel like you are leaving a lot out, my friend," Kiko said.

"I mean, I think you can fill in the blanks," Joey replied.

"Um, I think not!" Kiko pointed her long stiletto nail at Joey. "You've been very much secret-squirrel about you and Shane, and I know certain people have insider knowledge, but I need to know just a few more details."

"Like?"

"Like?" Kiko mimicked her. "I feel like Nicole, but I need to know how he went from being 'like your brother' to suggesting you be together. Even if I do admit that I knew you guys were friends with benefits at the very least, I'd still need to understand some shit."

"Hey," Nicole cried out at the reference. "I just like shit to make sense. Pardon me if I don't let people play in my face all day."

Joey threw her hands up. "Ok. Ok. What do you want to know?"

"Well... How did you guys become so close?" Kiko asked.

"Yeah. We all met around the same time, but when did you guys become a thing?" Nicole asked.

Joey thought about it for a moment. She remembered the moment she found out that Shane had feelings for her and knew she had real feelings for him.

Christmas Break – 2003 Freshman Year

The first holiday season without her grandmother was hard for Joey. She'd ignored Thanksgiving, which was easy enough because a lot of other students stayed on campus, but she was dreading Christmas break. She didn't feel like flying out to Oakland to experience the chaos that was her mother's house, and she didn't want to sit in the house in Louisiana alone. Shane was planning to go home, and she wasn't thrilled at the prospect of staying in the boys' dorm alone.

She was packing her stuff half-heartedly as she weighed her options. It wasn't that she didn't love her siblings because she did. She just knew her mother would use her being there as an opportunity to take time for herself, and Joey wasn't in the headspace for babysitting. Louisiana was looking more and more like her only real choice.

"What you pouting for, Shawty?" Shane always playfully flicked her lip when he caught her brooding.

"Just trying to decide if I'm going home or to my mother's, and it's looking more and more like home." She shrugged as she tossed a few more items in her suitcase.

"You're gonna go home and stay in that house alone?"

"It's either that or a house full of kids," she sighed.

"Hmm." Shane pondered her dilemma as he stuffed random things into his duffle bag.

"Why don't you come home with me?"

"To Georgia?"

"Naw. My dad is throwing some big ass Christmas party and wants me there."

"I thought you didn't really get along with your dad?"

"I don't, but he funds my entire life, so I don't fuss when he asks me to do shit. Besides, he throws dope parties. He's an entertainment lawyer, so he knows a lot of people."

"Wow. And he wouldn't mind? Are you sure?"

"I'm positive. Aunt Tori will be there, and there are enough rooms at his beach house. Trust me, you'll have fun."

Joey could feel her mood lifting. She considered his offer, not finding any real reason to turn it down. Her only concern was that he felt compelled to take care of her.

"Listen," she said, putting down whatever she was folding to pack next and turned to face him. "I don't want you to feel obligated to do this."

Shane just looked at her like she was being silly. "You know I don't do anything I don't want to do."

"That's true," she chuckled.

They were quiet after that. Things between them had been different since they hooked up. They hadn't done it again since, and both swore to each other that it was a one-time thing and that they didn't want to ruin their friendship, but instead of things being awkward, they seemed to be even more comfortable around each other. Sometimes, she caught him watching her, but for the most part, it was like it had never happened.

"So? Is that a yes?" He looked at her expectantly, and she smiled.

"Yeah. I'll go. Let me book my flight."

"No need. My dad is chartering me a jet."

"Oh? I know he's loaded, but damn!"

"Yeah. My parents like to spend money on me to make up for abandoning me my entire childhood."

"My dad is rich, but he uses his money like a weapon. I'd rather not even bother. Thank God my grandmother looked out for me the way she did. She always hated that he put restrictions and conditions on me when he wasn't even around to love on me."

"I wish I could have met her," Shane said with a small smile.

"She would have loved you," Joey replied. "She would have spoiled you and baked all your favorite treats."

"Can you bake like her?"

"I can hook you up with cookies and snacks, but the breads and fancy pastries are not my forte."

"Well, then you better hook me up with those butterscotch cookies, cause I been fiending for them. That'll be your payment for the trip," he laughed.

"Deal." They shook on it and continued their packing.

Joey was excited to fly on a private jet for the first time. She was in awe of the whole experience, from the all-black Escalade that came and picked them up, to the quick boarding, and the array of foods and drinks awaiting them on the plane. They spent the first half of the flight talking and joking until she fell asleep, and when she opened her eyes again they were already descending to John Wayne Airport.

They were both relatively quiet as the limo that picked them up drove them out to his father's house. The closer they got, the more Joey deduced the beach house was most likely a mansion, and she was right. When they pulled up to the gate of a home in the exclusive Laguna Beach neighborhood, her eyes almost popped out of her head. She tried to keep her composure as they exited the car in front of a three-level dream home.

"You actually live here?" She couldn't keep the wonderment out of her voice.

"My father lives here. I live in Georgia. Remember?"

"Right, but if you wanted to, you could live here?"

"My dad doesn't even live here. His main house is in L.A. He uses this place for special occasions, so I usually come when he's not here."

"That is crazy," she said in awe as they entered the foyer of the stately home.

An older gentleman in a tailored suit greeted them. "Hello, Shane. It's good to have you home."

"Hey, Allen. This is my friend, Joey. She'll be here with me for the holidays."

"Very nice to meet you, Joey. Will you be sharing a room?"

The question, though politely asked, caught them both off guard. Joey could feel the blush creep up her neck as both Shane and Allen awaited her answer.

"Uh, I –"

"No, Joey can stay in one of the guest rooms," Shane replied.

"Ah, ok," Allen replied. "I think she'll like the room next to yours. The view of the ocean is phenomenal."

"I agree. Can you have our bags put away while I give Joey a tour of the property?"

"Yes. And I'll have Estelle freshen her room. Good to have you with us, Miss Joey."

"Aww, thank you, Allen. And it's just Joey." She smiled at him before he nodded, and Shane tugged her toward the main living room.

"Was that the butler?" Joey whispered, ashamed that she was so impressed with the thought.

"I guess you can call it that. Allen and his wife Estelle care for the estate and manage all the employees."

"Wow," Joey replied. She had thought she was rich when she received that check from her grandmother's insurance policy, but now she felt poor again.

Shane gave her the grand tour, which revealed a house so stunning that Joey was afraid someone would jump out and tell her that she wasn't supposed to be there. It was a six-bedroom, beachfront property with each level having a wraparound patio facing the ocean. There was a pool, a theater room, a terrace grotto, and an outdoor fire pit. Joey couldn't wait to experience all there was to offer.

She spent the week exploring the estate and the surrounding neighborhood. Shane's best friend from high school, Damien, flew in for the party, too, so she indulged in a lot of alone time in the heated pool or by the beach. It was December, too cold to swim in the ocean, but she would walk in up to her calves and stare out at the horizon.

Shane Sr. was nothing like Joey expected. With how Shane described their relationship, she expected him to be cold and distant, but he wasn't that at all. Once he learned of Joey's situation and her grandmother's passing, he sat her down and helped her chart a course for her future. He even advised her on options to invest her inheritance. Half went into a high-yield savings account, she put some into bonds, and she cashed out thirty thousand to supplement her tuition and cushion her savings account.

Experiencing how Shane's father lived breathed new life into her vision for the future. She not only wanted to have a corporate career; she wanted to make a name for herself. She wanted to amass wealth and live in luxury. "The sky is the limit" was her new motto. Once again, her grandmother's advice helped bolster her determination to create the life of her dreams.

Sometimes, she'd hang with Shane and Damien while they watched old highlight reels of the NBA greats from the 80's and 90's. Shane was obsessed with Dennis Rodman, who was the same height and was known for his aggressive defensive style. Even though he was tall for a high school or college player, Shane knew that in the NBA, he'd most likely be a power forward instead of the center role he filled at FAMU unless he grew a few more inches. As it was, he made sure to sharpen his ball handling and long-distance shooting skills so that he would be a viable threat.

Seeing him so passionate and determined about his future excited Joey and gave her the idea to link their careers. If he did make it to the league, she wanted to have his back. They hadn't known each other long, but Joey had a feeling that he would play a significant role in her future. Maybe one day, if the stars aligned, they would be in a space where being a couple was an option. Until then, she was content with the status quo of their relationship.

It was strange to watch Shane and his father interact. Even though they weren't close, his dad took a keen interest in his education and athletic achievements. And when he learned of Joey's pursuit into public relations, he sat with her and gave her advice based on his business dealings. He also gave her contacts of women he knew in that field who would be willing to mentor her. Then Aunt Tori arrived and adopted Joey as her own.

Together, the two women went shopping and lunching and had long talks on the beach or by the fire pit when the evenings cooled down. It was one such night when Joey stepped away to take a call from her mother, and when she returned, she overheard Tori and Shane talking. Well, Tori did most of the talking, and Shane did most of the listening.

"So, I see you brought your girl with you," Tori said playfully.
"Joey and I are just friends," Shane replied with a shrug. Joey couldn't see his face because his back was turned, but she could see the skeptical expression on Tori's.
"Hmm," Tori hummed. "Your friend that you wish was more than your friend."
"C'mon," Shane chuckled.

"Seriously," Tori continued. "She's a beautiful girl, beautiful spirit. You don't play around with a woman like that, though. She's got too much fire in her. If you're just gonna be her friend, be her best friend. Let her be, don't try to play that possessive bullshit. Losing her grandmother and having no one to look out for her is rough enough without the added disappointment of relationship drama. You're both young. Truly allow her to be who she's gonna be and figure out who you are. Then, when the time is right, you become more."

As nosey as she was to know what he would say next, Joey was also terrified to hear what Shane felt about their future. Just hearing confirmation that he wanted more from her was a lot, and for a split second, she considered what it would be like to be with him in that way. The feeling in the pit of her stomach wasn't butterflies, though, and she felt her palms sweat. So, she released an exaggerated sigh, alerting them to her return.

"My mother is so ridiculous," she huffed. "Do you know she's upset that I'm in California but not visiting her in Oakland? Like it's right around the corner. The fact that she thinks I'm poor and is giving me a hard time about buying a plane ticket is wild."

"I'm sorry to hear that," Tori said, patting the seat next to her for Joey to join her. "Your mom might not be handling Grann's death that well."

"Nope. She's always been this way. Sadly." Joey leaned on Tori's shoulder as the older woman stroked her hair. Shane just shook his head as he watched the comfortable interaction between Joey and his aunt. For once, Joey found that she couldn't read him, and wondered if he was still thinking about what Tori had said.

Joey was on edge on the day of the party because she didn't know what to expect. She also wasn't sure the dresses she had packed would be good enough to mingle with the elite guest list of invitees. She was weighing her outfit choices when Tori stuck her head in the ajar room door.

"Hey, Shawty." Tori used the unofficial nickname that Shane called her. "What are you up to?"

"I'm trying to decide what to wear tonight. How dressed up do I need to be? I don't want to be embarrassed." Joey slumped onto the plush bedding, unused to feeling so out of place.

"I know you're not over there pouting," Tori placed her hands on her hips. "First of all, you make the clothes; the clothes don't make you. You betta start behaving like you know your damn worth, even if you're wearing rags. Your confidence and personality make you even more attractive than those pretty looks. You hear me?"

"Yes, Tori," Joey smiled.

"But if you're that worried about it, you can come with me to the mall, and then we can do each other's hair when we get back."

"Oh my God! Can we?"

"Uh, I'm pretty sure that's what I just said," Tori said as she snapped for Joey to get with it.

The deep burgundy dress that Tori helped pick out suited Joey's tawny complexion to perfection. Paired with fresh honey-blonde highlights and a bold, dark lip, Joey embraced her dark feminine side. She walked into the party, turning heads and ignoring the attention as if she was used to it. Tori may or may not have advised her on how to move about the crowd, but Joey was feeling herself. She looked so good that Shane was stunned when he first saw her. He had to do a double take because he didn't recognize her at first, with her curls straightened into a sleek, straight look.

Despite the party being for his father's friends and celebrity clients, there were a few people Joey and Shane's age sprinkled throughout. A few were the older children of guests, and a few knew Shane from his years of visiting since he was a kid. Soon, they all congregated in his father's cigar room, where he kept his fine cigars, expensive liquor, and extensive record collection of old-school classics dating back to the 50's. The room was usually off-limits, but Shane knew his father would be too busy to care. So, the group snuck a few drinks while he played records.

When the night wound down, only Joey, Shane, and Damien were left lounging on the patio with the warmth from the heat lamps that lined the length of the balcony to keep them comfortable. Joey was standing at the patio railing, looking out at the dark expanse of the ocean, while the boys debated which Batman was the most iconic. She vaguely heard Damien saying goodnight, and then Shane was at her side. "Wildflower" by The New Birth played, and she found herself getting lost in the lyrics.

"Can you believe I hardly danced tonight? And I love to dance," she sighed.

"Dance with me?" Shane leaned against the railing next to her with a hand extended in invitation.

Joey looked up at him, still towering over her despite her heels, and noticed how handsome he looked. He tamed his hair with curling gel, and the tips were dyed platinum. She also noticed the new piercing and earring he was wearing; a large diamond stud in the first hole, and a diamond-encrusted cross in the new hole. Shane's style was different. He mixed elements of rock star wild with hip-hop fashion.

She took his hand, and he assumed the closed position with both their arms up and out to the side. At first, they just did the basic back-

and-forth steps, but as the song played and the weight of the lyrics settled over them, Shane pulled her into his arms, and Joey rested her head against his chest. They danced in silence, both their hearts beating fast, but neither wanted to ruin the mood.

Afterward, they walked to the wing of the house where their bedrooms were. Hand in hand. Joey's mind was racing a mile a minute with thoughts that conflicted with her feelings. She knew they had sworn to be friends, but she wanted him to kiss her more than anything. Thoughts of the night they hooked up constantly flashed through her mind. How gentle yet passionate he was with her. How he had slid down her body and delivered her first oral orgasm, and how he filled her so completely that it felt like he was a part of her.

When they arrived at her door, they both paused but said nothing. Shane toyed with her hair, tucking her silk press behind her ears while she fiddled with the zipper of his leather Members Only jacket. When they made eye contact, Joey felt a heat radiating throughout her entire body. Shane's eyes dilated as they stared at each other, then he leaned in and kissed her forehead, then her ear, then her cheek.

"Shane," she sighed. "I thought we agreed just to be friends." Her words sounded weak, even to her own ears.

"Friends can kiss, right?" He kissed her nose, brushing his lips across her soft skin.

"Uh," she uttered, full of skepticism but also hoping that he would just do it.

"Just consider it a friendly kiss," he murmured before sealing her mouth with his.

Joey snaked her arms around his neck as she kissed him back. Their tongues warred, and teeth noshed at each other's lips as the kiss grew heated. Joey couldn't help the needy whimpers that escaped her throat as her fingers weaved through his hair. His body pressed against hers until her back was flush with her bedroom door. She could feel his hard length pressing into her while his hands slid up and down her back.

Tori's voice approaching in the distance snapped them out of their lust-filled stupor. Joey pushed Shane away, giggling at his shocked expression as she ducked into her room. He reached his and closed the door just as Tori hit the corner to their hallway. Joey was still breathing hard when her phone dinged with a message.

Shane: That wasn't very friendly
Joey: Neither was that kiss
Shane: But you enjoyed it
Joey: I cannot tell a lie
Shane: That's what friends are for
Joey: Hmm... I don't kiss Nicole like that
Shane: I'm your special friend ☐
Joey: Go to bed
Shane: I'd rather come to yours
Joey: Shane!
Shane: May I come over?

Joey: No
Shane: Why?
Joey: I don't want things to get all weird
Shane: I swear to God I won't get weird
Joey: This is the last time
Shane: Or, maybe a Christmas tradition?
Joey: Come on already!
Shane: I'm cumming

Chapter 9

Present

"So, we've got some big news," Stew, Joey's director, announced at the head of the conference table as he re-read information on the biggest clients in their firm.

"Joey," he glanced at her with a proud smirk. "You've got your work cut out with Shane Duncan, but it looks like you're doing a good job reeling in this bad boy phase or whatever he's going through. Rich life crisis, if you ask me."

There were chuckles from a few of her co-workers who agreed with his assessment. It was known that Shane came from a privileged background, so the numerous headlines of his excessive partying and womanizing just seemed like a young guy with too much money at his disposal. Joey knew the truth but wasn't at liberty to share it with her team. She also knew they didn't really give a damn, but that's another story. Her job was to clean up the mess he made of his reputation so that he could get picked up by the team he wanted to be on and not be seen as a liability.

"I've got it under control," she replied confidently.

"I'm sure you do," Stew tossed back. "I trust you to get him ready for free agency. I have it on good authority that The Clippers are looking at him."

She simply nodded. Part of her process was keeping her methods to herself, and everyone knew better than to ask. There were whispers of how close she and Shane actually were, but Dante and Kelly kept people at bay. As planned.

Joey wasn't even surprised when her phone vibrated with a message from the topic of conversation. He was also supposed to give her an important update.

"This is Shane. I'll take it in my office," Joey said as she answered the call. "Hey. Give me a sec to get back to my office."

"Cool," Shane's low tone replied.

Joey hit the long hallway to her corner office at a brisk stride. Once inside, she closed the door behind her and slid into her leather recliner, kicking off her heels.

"Wassap," she said less formally now that she didn't have an audience.

"Nothin', man. I just got out of my initial negotiations."

"And?" She was impatient to hear what the outcome was. Stew was behind the eight-ball, as usual. That's why Joey was the star of the firm. It didn't hurt that some of her biggest clients were also some of her closest friends.

"The Clippers want to make an offer," he said with pride.

"Shut up," she squealed, then remembered where she was and lowered to a hushed tone. "Are you serious? You're coming to L.A.?"

"Well, Remy and Chelle are flying out to negotiate, as usual, but it's basically a done deal. They want me, and Phoenix isn't prepared to match their offer."

"Wow... You really did it! I can't believe it."

"We did it," he corrected her.

"Yes, we did," she said with a smile.

"You know, when we were in FAM and agreed to work together to accomplish our dreams, I didn't really believe you. At first. But after I saw how you killed every goal you set your mind to, I decided to trust you. You've always had my back."

"Oh, so you didn't believe in me, huh?"

"I mean," he chuckled. "You were sleeping in my dorm room because it was safer than that shady motel you were attempting to live out of. Your decision-making was questionable at best."

"Whatever, Shane! That should have shown you how determined I was. Jerk!"

He laughed. "No, but for real. We have to celebrate with the gang when everything is officially inked."

"Definitely."

"I miss you," he said in a different, deeper tone.

"Oh really? Not getting enough action out in Arizona?"

"Stop. You know half that shit they report isn't even true."

"No? So, you've only ran through a quarter of the women in Phoenix. Got it."

"Joey."

"Shane," she replied. Dead serious.

"What perfume are you wearing?"

"Shane," she repeated in a dismissive tone.

"Is it the one I like? Smells all musky with a hint of sweetness."

"Shane, please."

"Like some sort of exotic berry."

"Please," she said again, but she was smiling.

"Then it mixes with your scent, and *mmm*," he groaned deeply as if the memory was real.

"Will you stop? I'm at work."

Specific memories were flooding her mind and causing another flood between her thighs. It had always been that way with him. One minute, they'd be laughing and joking, and the next, clothes were coming off. She had tried her best not to blur the lines with him, but it wasn't easy. Especially when he called her and started talking in that sexy timbre that let her know exactly how he was feeling.

Now, there was no point in trying.

"Every time you wear that, I just want to eat you. Lick you everywhere."

"Shane, behave. I'm at work," she pleaded, squeezing her thighs together.

"I bet your pussy is nice and juicy right now," he murmured.

"I'm gonna hang up on you," she warned.

"I know it is. You stay wet. Huh? My little peach."

When she didn't reply, he chuckled. "Tell me how wet I make you, baby."

"Why are you doing this?"

"You wanna touch yourself so bad right now. Don't you?"

"Yes," she sighed. Finally giving in to him.

"Do it, baby. I know you're wearing one of those little skirts that show off your sexy ass legs. Slip your hand under your desk and past those lace panties you're wearing."

Joey's only response was a whimper. She hated that he had that effect on her. Her hand was already gripping the edge of her skirt, and her eyes darted to the blinds on the glass pane next to her office door. It showed the path to the conference room on the other end of the hall, and no one would see her unless they were just about to enter her office. She could get away with a quick session.

"You're thinking about it, huh?"

"Mhm," she moaned lightly.

"Come on," he goaded her. What are you waiting for?"

Her eyes were closed as she allowed herself a moment to decide if she would go through with it. She knew her pussy would be leaky and throbbing until she handled what he started. The timbre of his voice was stirring up all types of raunchy memories that were inciting a riot in between her thighs. Her pussy was throbbing like it hadn't been touched in years.

"You look so sexy when you're turned on. Your lips get all pouty, and your eyes slant just slightly. Especially when it's been a long time. You miss me?"

"Yes," she purred.

"Good girl," he said before hanging up.

Joey glared at her phone in disbelief, so stunned that he left her hanging that it caught her off guard that her office door was opening. She shrieked excitedly when her eyes registered that Shane was actually there in the flesh. Jumping up, she ran to greet him, ducking her head into the hallway to ensure no one was around before she shut her door, locked it, and closed her blinds.

"I can't stand you," she said as she grasped the lapel of his suit jacket and pulled him toward her. Shane smirked down at her as he snaked one arm up her back and grasped the back of her neck.

"I know we don't have a lot of time, and I need to taste you. Right now," he said, running his hands up through her scalp and gripping her hair before pulling her head back. Joey's lips parted to say something, but he was already pressing his mouth to hers, his tongue seeking hers. He walked her backward until the backs of her thighs bumped against the edge of her desk. With his free hand, he pushed her laptop and various items on her desk to the side and hoisted her onto it.

"You're not even going to pretend to protest this time?"

"No," she panted. Her hands were already roaming up and down his long torso, settling on his belt buckle and undoing it.

"Aww, I kinda like it when you put up a fight," he grinned.

"You play too much," she replied. "My panties are probably ruined right now."

"Let me check," he replied.

Crouching down, he gripped her hip with one hand while the other slid up her leg from her calf to the V where her panties began. He pushed two fingers to her center to encounter what he knew would be soaking wet lace. Leaning forward, he pushed up her skirt, and pressed his face into her crotch and inhaled deeply, letting out a satisfied groan. Joey moaned in response and opened her legs wider, leaning back on her elbows.

Face still in the place, Shane began to tease her, letting his tongue lick at her sensitive spot through the delicate fabric. Taking his time, he gripped the lace edges and pulled them off. Then he stuffed them in his pants pocket. Next, he placed soft kisses against the smooth skin of her long legs, stopping to pay special attention behind her knees as one thumb explored her warm, drenched pussy.

Joey watched him intently. It turned her on even more how turned on he seemed to be with every inch of her, the way he lovingly kissed her ankle or how he didn't miss a spot, like behind her knees. He knew every inch of her body and what she liked.

That's why they couldn't stay away from each other. They understood each other too well. No one had been able to replace the other. Joey loved that Shane had an intuitive connection with her body, always able to decode her moods and desires.

He knew when she wanted it rough, when she needed a soft touch, or when she was in the mood for kink and adventure. For Shane, it was Joey's willingness to let him explore, to push the boundaries, and love every step of the way. He'd met other girls who claimed they were freaks or said they were down for whatever, but when it came down to it, they had all sorts of rules and restrictions. Things they weren't willing or ready to try. It wasn't a turn-off; it just made Joey that much more attractive to him.

As he quickly brought her to the brink with his tongue, he paused just as she began to tremble under his touch. Shane licked his lips, their eyes still glued to each other, and reached down to undo his zipper and release his erection with one hand as the other gripped and squeezed the plumpness of her hips. His fingertip traced over the simple heart outline tattoo that stood out on her light skin.

Joey squirmed and sighed, impatient for him to be inside her. Despite her reluctance to answer the question, she had missed Shane, and she'd grown tired of them being apart. Now that things were working out as planned, she always seemed desperate for him. And the added thrill of almost getting caught was turning her on.

"Shane," she whimpered, barely able to wait any longer.
"Yes, baby." His seductive voice made her quiver.
"Fuck me," she demanded.

Shane grinned as he complied. Pulling her to standing, he guided her toward the door, placed her hands above her head and pulled her hips back. He had a prime view of anyone coming down her hall and of her luscious ass.
"Arch your back."
Joey did as he said, bristling with anticipation.
"I've been thinking about being inside you," he whispered against her skin, his fingers spreading her open.
"Why?"
"You know why," he murmured.

"Tell me," she gasped as the initial thrust caught her off guard.

Shane groaned in ecstasy as she began to undulate against him. "Every time feels like the first time with you," he hissed.

"I love feeling you inside me," Joey moaned.

"Ah," he grunted. "Keep moving that ass. Just like that."

His grasp on her hip tightened as he slid the other arm around her torso, holding her tighter. He pressed his face into her hair, deeply inhaling her fresh scent before planting soft kisses against her ears and cheek. Joey whimpered at his tenderness while he fucked her hard up against the door. It was meant to be quick and dirty, but somehow, Shane always found a way to express his affection for her.

"I've missed you, baby. Missed this pussy. Missed those little sounds you make when you're trying to hold back. Don't hold back. Come for me."

Shane slid his hand around her throat, squeezing ever so lightly, knowing the effect it would have on her.

Joey loved rough sex, so that little gesture was enough to send her spiraling.

"Ahh," she moaned as her back arched, and she chased his thrusts, backing it up on him like her life depended on it. The light clapping sound of skin against skin sent Shane into a tailspin.

"Shit," he hissed as his orgasm followed right behind hers. His vision blurred for a moment, but he made sure to keep an eye out for any unsuspecting visitors.

They both huffed and panted, fighting to regain their composure. Shane eased out of Joey, pressing a hand to her mid back to keep her still as he watched his cum leak out of her.

"What are you doing?"

"I'm watching my creampie," he joked.

"Oh, my God!" She groaned. "You are so sick."

"I bet if I took a picture of it, you'd want to see it."

"You better send it to me!"

He chuckled, grabbing his phone out of his pocket to do just that.

"Why are you so nasty?" She giggled when he finally let her up to straighten her clothes after using a few of her wet wipes to clean them up. Joey kept a vigilant eye on her hallway, especially since Shane couldn't exactly sneak into the office incognito. She was surprised that someone hadn't found a reason to stop by.

"Why didn't you tell me you were already in the city so I could coordinate a room?"

"I wanted to surprise you, obviously," he replied.

"I just can't believe it's really all coming together," she mused.

Shane flashed a big smile, presenting her with his hand so they could do their signature handshake.

"It's me and you, babe."

"Yeah," Joey sighed. Some of her enthusiasm seemed to wane. Shane tilted his head as he regarded her mood change.

"You still haven't spoken to Dante?"

A guilty expression spreads across her face.

"I thought I had time," she whined when he growled with frustration. "I wanted to talk to him when he returned from Ghana, but he extended his trip. Probably found some pussy that was real good to him."

"Doubt it," Shane countered. "If he's actually sleeping with anyone else, much less spending money to do so, I'd be surprised."

"You're probably right," she returned. "But the fact is, he's not back yet. I can't break up with him over the phone."

"You could," he quipped. "But that's foul as hell."

"Right. Which is why I'm waiting. But since you're giving me shit," Joey shot him a pointed look as she perched on her desk. "What's up with Kelly? Isn't your breakup on the horizon? Why has she been posting so much lovey-dovey content?"

Shane breathed a frustrated sigh and folded his arms across his chest as he leaned against the office door.

"I need to fly down and see her. I told her to ease up on that shit, but she was talking about us extending things. Like that's her call to make."

"What do you mean, extending things?" Joey flashed him with an skeptical glare. "What point of temporary is she missing? Please don't tell me you actually fucked her?"

When Shane's answer wasn't forthcoming, Joey groaned. "Are you kidding me?"

"Oh, come on. Don't give me that," he tossed back. "I know it was a deal, but it's not like I didn't have any feelings for her. Spending all that time together..." His words trailed off because there wasn't much to explain.

"This better not blow up in your face," Joey warned.

"Like I said. It's as good as over. We have a couple more events to attend. The signing announcement falls within Kelly's contract, so she's gonna have to be there, but after that, we just have to have the official talk and get her signature."

"Ok." Joey folded her arms across her chest, clearly not as excited as before.

"Come here," he said, pulling her in for another hug. "Don't worry. I got this. I got you."

December 2003 / Freshman Year

"Wheelz of Steel" by Outkast blasted through the speakers in Shane's dorm room as he and Joey studied for an upcoming English final. It just happened that they both enjoyed listening to music while they studied or did homework. Joey sat at the computer desk while Shane had his books and papers sprawled across his bed. He nodded to the beat while singing along to his favorite rap group. It was his turn to pick the music, and he put on a playlist of their greatest hits.

"Do you love Outkast because they're dope? Or because they're from ATL?" Joey asked when he ran the song back.

"Probably both," he said after some thought. "I mean, you can't front that they put Atlanta on the map, but they had me hooked from ATLiens."

"I feel you. I'm a Lil Wayne loyalist. For life." She threw up some pseudo-gang sign for emphasis, causing him to laugh.

"Ok, you got that. I'm down with the Hot Boyz, too. I'm for anyone who puts a spotlight on the South. It's about time we got some shine."

"Don't let Chelle and Nicole hear you say that," she joked.

"Man, please. NY had hip-hop in a chokehold for so damn long. They can't be mad. And I've seen them both dancin' to our Dirty South bangers."

They continued to talk and work, only taking breaks to eat. Joey had been staying with him in his room since her grandmother's death. Just like he'd said, neither the coaches nor the other players gave him a hard time, especially since she was part of the Cheer squad, their honorary sisters. Shane being the star player on the team didn't hurt either.

Everyone just looked the other way.

Shane was humming along to "The Way You Move" when his phone pinged with a special ringtone. Joey knew from experience that it was Kelly, his ex-girlfriend from high school. Like clockwork, she called almost every night to talk to him before bed. Well, maybe Kelly's bedtime because Shane was a night owl, and he and Joey would be up talking and watching movies until the wee hours. It irked Joey that Shane claimed Kelly meant nothing to him, yet he seemed to jump whenever she called.

Joey didn't understand why it bothered her so much. It's not like she and Shane were together. She'd made her stance on relationships very clear when they first met, and he'd agreed. His sights were set on the NBA, and he wasn't trying to do anything that would cause him to lose focus. It was more about the fact that he talked to Joey about damn near everything, like she was one of the guys, but was never forthcoming about his ex.

"I'll be back," he tossed over his shoulder as he took the call out in the lounge.

Joey knew she shouldn't feel jealous. She shouldn't feel any way at all, but she felt a weird feeling in the pit of her belly. Grann's words crossed her mind, and she felt a pang of nostalgia for her grandmother. It had only been a couple of months since her funeral, and the sadness was still raw. Joey blamed her strange reaction to Shane's calls with Kelly, on that.

By the time he returned to the room, she had already showered and was ready for bed. She tried not to look at him, not wanting to give off a weird vibe, but true to the nature of their budding friendship, he picked up on it anyway.

"What's up?" He watched her as she put her homework away, obviously avoiding eye contact.
"Nothing," she said without looking up.
"It doesn't seem like nothing. Your whole mood done changed. You good?"
"I'm fine. How's Kelly?"

She hated herself as soon as she said it. The last thing she wanted him to think was that she was jealous in any way. Shane seemed to be taken aback and didn't respond right away. He watched her continue her bedtime routine, realizing that she was serious. When she continued to avert her eyes, he walked over to her.

"Hey." He took her books out of her hand and placed them on her desk, then slid his finger under her chin to force her to look up at him. "What's the matter?"

"Honestly," she sighed. "I don't know."
"But it's something?"
"Why do you leave the room whenever you talk to Kelly? You don't care if I hear what you and Jay talk about or your boys from back home. Even when your mother or aunt calls."

Shane's eyebrows went sky-high at her question. "I mean. I don't know. Our conversations are dry and goofy."

"So? If she's not your girl, what do you have to hide?"

"I didn't think I was hiding. Just wanted a little privacy. I mean, sometimes we flirt or whatever."

"Oh," Joey gasped, feeling like she might be imposing on him for the first time. He had insisted she stay with him, and they had such a good time with each other she never thought that she was invading his space.

"I'm sorry. I guess I could hang out with the girls more or find a better apartment now that I have money."

"That's not what I meant," he said—stopping her from turning away. "You're not bothering me, and I want you here. Kelly was my first, and I guess I still play up on that. She treats me like a superstar, so I give her the attention she wants. It's a habit, but trust me, I don't want her."

"You don't have to explain," she replied. "I shouldn't have even said anything. It's not that serious."

"I don't want you to be upset. Are we good?"

"We're good," she replied, initiating their special handshake.

A little while later, they were both in their respective beds, and the lights were off. The TV was on Nick at Night, Shane's favorite channel to fall asleep to, and one of Grann's favorite shows came on. Before Joey knew what was happening, she felt the tears slipping down her cheek. Dabbing at her eyes, she tried to get herself under control, but the tears kept streaming, and she attempted to stifle her sniffles.

"Joey?"

"I'm fine. I'm sorry."

"What happened?" He sat up in his bed and stared at her, trying to make out her face from the glow of the TV. "Why are you crying?"

"This was one of Grann's favorite shows," she sniffed.

Without responding, Shane whipped back his covers and patted his mattress for her to join him. His bed was bigger, and he figured it was better to invite her than to force himself on her. Although she hesitated, Joey left her bed and crawled into his. They adjusted their positions until he was the big spoon, and she was the little spoon. He pulled the blankets around them because the winter night was brisk, even for Florida, and held her to his chest.

He didn't speak because he wasn't sure what to say to comfort her. She was quiet because she didn't know how to articulate not only her sadness but also how she felt all alone in the world. That's part of the reason she enjoyed staying with Shane. Their friendship, as unorthodox and unexpected as it was, meant a lot to her. The fact that he didn't make her feel uncomfortable in any way was a blessing. Most guys would have done or said something inappropriate by that point, but other than their conversation about Kelly, he was like hanging with a brother or a cousin.

But there was something about lying against his chest that made her feel different. Even though everyone called him skinny, there was a solidness to his form that made her feel secure. He smelled like the lemon and sage body wash she had bought him, mixed with his natural scent that she had come to love. She felt herself growing warm and found that she was very aware of her own breathing. So many synapses were firing off in her body, and sleep was the furthest thing from her mind.

She wondered if he was as affected by her as she was by him. Instinctively, she shifted and was met by a long, hard erection poking her back. Freezing up, she held her breath. Her curiosity intensified because he'd kept his attraction to her under wraps. Of course, she had seen how he checked her out when they first met, and even caught a few glances the first couple of days of class, but nothing more.

His arm around her tightened, and he kissed the back of her head, but that was it. He didn't press his hard-on into her or make any other advances. Joey damn near stopped breathing as she waited patiently to see if he'd make a move. Didn't all guys do something when their dick got hard? For all her waiting, he just continued to hold her.

And for some reason, that turned her on even more. She turned in his arms, throwing a leg over his thigh. The fluorescent glow from the television highlighted his cheekbones and fringed eyelashes, and she traced his features as if seeing them for the first time. His eyes remained closed, but he leaned into her touch. A sharp ache between her legs and latent desire rippling through her body caused her to clench her thighs. Shane gripped her hips with his fingers digging into her flesh through her pajama pants. Her body was wound so tight she thought she would splinter into a million pieces if he didn't touch her.

Scooting upwards, she placed her lips against his for a gentle kiss, just letting them rest against his. Shane's eyes blinked open, and she could see the lust burning within them. With a tentative nod, he leaned down to kiss her back. Their eyes locked until Joey moaned, and Shane closed his, overcome by the tempting sound. Then, in an instant, he had her on her back, pinned beneath him.

"Joey." He uttered her name like a plea. "I'm trying to be good."

"Stop trying," she whispered against the racing pulse point in his neck.

Her hands slid under his T-shirt and up and down his back. When she felt goosebumps erupt under her touch, it spurred her on. She let her nails lightly score his skin as she continued to explore his back and arms, pulling off his shirt. The tattoo around his neck always fascinated her so she began to place light kisses all around the crowned points.

"Joey," he moaned when she began to lick and suck, and then hissed when she nipped his skin.

"Mmm," she hummed against his skin.

He snaked his fingers through her hair and cradled the back of her head, kissing her with a hunger that made her dizzy. Their uncertain exploration of each other shifted to a fierce need to touch each other everywhere. Months of pent-up emotions spilled out, and they clutched at each other for comfort. Even with their connection's playfulness, an undercurrent of heavy attraction drew them together.

Shane began peeling away her pajamas while kissing and exploring every new expanse of exposed skin he encountered. Joey's hands continued to touch him everywhere until she was toying with the waistband of his basketball shorts. They were on the precipice of curiosity and exploration, knowing that going any further would take them to another level.

Shane kissed Joey until her lips felt swollen and bruised. Their bodies strained together, their breathing became synchronized, and her core was throbbing out of control.

"Shane," she whimpered when his hips began to gyrate. The bulge of his arousal pressed against her center, and she arched her back so that her clit could feel the contact. Without even thinking, she slid her hand down to caress his erection. His hips bucked at the contact, and he groaned when she began to stroke him.

"Damn... I want to be inside you so bad. You want to feel me?"
"Yes," Joey moaned, her legs spreading wide at the suggestion.
"You sure?"
"Yes."

She loved that he wanted to be cautious, but it was too late for all that. That night, things between them changed forever.

Present

It was the night of the signing celebration for Shane joining the L.A. Clippers, and Joey was feeling a level of excitement that she hadn't in a long time. Not only were they finally in the same city, but Chelle also confirmed that she and Remy were looking at homes in the Los Angeles area. Jay was most likely also going to sign with the Clippers when his contract was up in Italy, and Dom was in negotiations to sign with a Cali team.

It had always been Joey's dream to have the gang together on the same coast, at the very least.

She spent the day with Chelle shopping and preparing for the event. It was the official team welcoming, so the crowd wouldn't be too large, but she had another party planned that the whole crew would attend. That night, it would just be Chelle and Remy since they both represented Shane in some capacity, and all of Joey's office because the NBA teams were known for their lavish events.

She caught a reflection of herself in the mirrored wall of the elevator of the venue that was hosting the party, and she was practically glowing. The thought that they would soon be able to be out in the open and give their relationship a chance was a happiness that she had denied herself of ever believing could be. All the years that she had tried to convince herself that he was just a friend, but he was the man who felt like magic that her grandmother spoke of. A feeling that scared her so much that she ran from it.

Stepping off the elevator, she braced herself for one last night of pretending. Kelly would be there, as planned, and Joey had to steel herself to deal with the optics. Cleaning up his image had been a major factor in getting Shane signed to the team, so despite the stupid contract he signed with her, Kelly was good for his image. Of course, Joey hated to admit it.

When she walked in, the crowd was already buzzing. The party was composed of the team, so a few die-hard female fans were sprinkled in, as well as the owners, her office, and friends and family. It was a decent turnout, and the food and drinks were already flowing. Joey spotted Chelle and Remy at the end of the bar, and she headed in their direction. Shane was a few feet away, chatting with the owner and a couple of his new teammates.

"Hey guys." Joey greeted both of her friends with a big hug because it was her first time seeing them since their wedding. "You both look so married!"

"Is it crazy that I feel married?" Chelle asked.

"In a good way, I hope." Remy kissed his wife on the forehead, and she simpered up at him.

"In the best way," Chelle replied.

"Oh boy. I'm gonna need one of these," Joey said while snagging a glass of champagne off a passing tray.

"Let us enjoy our honeymoon phase," Remy chuckled.

"Please," Joey huffed playfully. "I doubt that's ending any time soon. If ever!"

"What's up, guys?" Shane joined them, throwing an arm around Joey and kissing her cheek before standing beside Remy. It took everything in her not to smile up at him like a stark, raving fool, even though they did exchange a quick glance and a smile. What she felt inside matched the googly eyes that Chelle was giving her husband.

"I'm so proud of you, Shane," Chelle gushed. "I can't say it enough."

"Thanks, Chelle. I couldn't have done it without you guys. Especially Joey."

"Aww, I was just doing my job." She actually blushed.

Before she could respond, a newcomer to the group interrupted their conversation.

"Sorry I'm late, babe," Kelly panted. She was still wearing her coat and looked like she'd just rushed in from the airport.

"You haven't missed anything yet," Shane said, placing a chaste kiss on her cheek.

"Hey, Chelle and Remy. Congratulations again. Sorry I couldn't make it to the wedding, but I hope you got my card," Kelly said, greeting them both with a hug. Then, almost like an afterthought, "Hello, Joey."

"Hello, Kelly," Joey returned her dry tone.

The two women stared each other down until Shane broke the silence.

"Well, now that we're all here, I guess we can let the franchise do their thing." He stepped back and had a brief conversation with the owners, who nodded and stepped forward to begin the welcome speech.

The entire vibe of the room seemed to change upon Kelly's arrival. Her awkward greeting didn't help, and the strange way she kept tugging on her coat was distracting. Joey wondered if she'd done something silly, like show up naked underneath to try to entice him. Little did she know that Joey had a suite rented for her and Shane to spend the night. Kelly would be going back to her hotel alone.

The owner's announcement was relatively quick. Then Remy and Chelle said their congratulations, and then Joey and her C.E.O. After everyone said their piece, Shane stepped to the podium to deliver his thank you speech. When he was winding down, Kelly stepped up next to him to add her two cents. Chelle and Joey exchanged side-eyes, wondering what she had to say.

"I just want to say congratulations to Shane. The future holds so much in store for us." Kelly smiled at him as she opened her coat, revealing that she was pregnant.

"Did you know about this?" Chelle asked under her breath, and all Joey could do was nod no.

It felt like the walls were closing in around her. There was even a slight ringing in her right ear as she watched Kelly rub the surprise baby bump she had just revealed. Joey felt her heart rate increasing as she tried to keep the smile plastered on her face, but she felt like she was turning in on herself or her insides were fighting to come out. Glancing around the room to all the happy faces and cheers of congratulations made her feel even smaller as her entire future seemed to slip away right before her eyes.

To his credit, Shane didn't look excited about the revelation that he was about to be a father, but when he pulled Kelly into his arms for a hug, Joey felt herself losing it. Placing her un-sipped glass of champagne on the nearest table, she turned and made a beeline for the restroom. She'd had a panic attack before, but this wasn't that. This was more like a rage attack where she felt like she would combust if she didn't let it out. There wasn't any putting on a brave face or pretending that she was happy for him.

Bursting into the women's restroom and finding it empty, she doubled over as a small, mangled cry escaped her lips, and she gasped for air. She didn't even realize she'd been holding her breath. Still having some presence of mind, she skulked forward toward the stalls, checking each one to ensure she was truly alone before she broke down. The tears came in a furious torrent as she cried, low sobs that emanated from the pit of her stomach. She hunched over again as the pain seemed to try to break her physically.

The door to the entrance swung open, and Chelle rushed in before Joey could even attempt to contain herself.

"Oh my God," Chelle whispered when she heard the anguish in Joey's cry. "Joey? Honey, talk to me. What's going on?" She froze in her tracks at the unexpected sight of her friend's unraveling.

Chelle had seen the life drain from Joey's face when Kelly announced her pregnancy and knew something was off. She knew there was something more to the relationship with Shane, but she had no idea how deep.

"I can't," Joey whimpered through her weeping. Chelle approached her tentatively, not sure how to calm her. She placed a hand on Joey's lower back and an arm around her shoulder, hoping to get her upright. "How could he do this to me?"

The tortured look in Joey's eyes hurt Chelle's heart. "Try to calm down, babe. Breathe. It's going to be ok."
"No," Joey sobbed. "You don't understand–"

Shane barged into the already small room, his tall, imposing figure seeming to suck up whatever space was left. He looked frantic, and seeing the state that Joey was in, he rushed toward her.
"Joey? Baby, please don't cry. It's not–"
"Don't cry?" Joey screamed. "Just get out, Shane. Get away from me." She pushed him away as he tried to pull her from Chelle's embrace.
"Hold on a second," Chelle whispered, hoping Joey would follow suit. "Joey, calm down. Shane, please back off." She pleaded with her eyes, hoping he was sane enough to listen to her.
"Joey. I swear I didn't know she was pregnant. I didn't plan this. I don't even know how it happened."

"Just shut the fuck up! I don't want to hear any of your excuses. Leave me alone."

Shane shook his head, hands in prayer mode, as he tried to get her to see him. "Come on, Joey. You know me. Please talk to me."

"Leave!" The depth and bass in Joey's demand frightened Chelle and shut Shane up. "Just go."

"I don't even know how this happened," he gritted.

"You fucked her raw, Shane. That's how it happened," Joey yelled back.

"You're the only person I've ever fucked raw. You know that."

"Jesus Christ," Chelle muttered in astonishment. She'd never seen so much passion or fire from either of her two friends, and she was at a loss on how to mediate the situation.

"Shane, I think you need to get back out there before someone comes looking for you. You two can talk when you've both calmed down."

"I'm so over this shit. Don't bother calling me." Joey's eyes shot daggers at Shane as she pointed at him.

Chelle stopped him before he could respond. "Shane, go!"

Shane seemed hesitant, but Chelle glared at him and pointed at the door.

"It's not what you think, Joey," he said in one last desperate attempt to reach her.

"Go," Chelle yelled, stomping her foot for emphasis.

"Joey, I love you."

The resulting scream that Joey released was as blood-curdling as it was unintelligible. Chelle gasped, covering her mouth in shock as she tried to figure out how to calm her friend down. She looked at Shane and motioned for him to leave since he seemed to be the contributing factor in Joey's madness. He gripped the tips of his curls like he wanted to rip his hair out as he backed away, but he didn't say anything.

Chelle glared at him until he turned, snatched the door open and stormed out.

Placing both hands on Joey's shoulders, Chelle tried to reason with her. "Joey, breathe, babe. That's it. Take breaths." She nodded as Joey attempted to do what she had said. It took a minute, with a few errant whimpers and broken sobs breaking free, but Joey eventually stopped crying.

"I'm sorry," she sniffed, dabbing her nose.

"What the hell is going on?" Chelle was afraid to let Joey go, fearing she would fall apart again.

"I need to get out of here," Joey replied, sounding panicked again.

"I think you need to calm down a little bit more," Chelle suggested. "Let's fix your makeup, then I'll have Remy bring our coats. But give me a clue– I mean, I think I know why you're upset, but not why you're acting insane."

"I'll explain everything to you. I just need to get out of here. If I see either Shane or Kelly, I might snap. For real."

Chelle nodded, grabbing her phone and texting Remy to meet them by the restrooms. She watched Joey closely as she attempted to fix her makeup in the mirror. The way her friend's eyes continued to tear up despite saying she was fine and kept getting a faraway look made her sad. In all the years they'd been friends, she'd never seen Joey that emotional. She was the one who usually cheered everyone else up.

To see her so distraught was shocking.

"Done." Joey tried to impart an air of "having it together" in her tone, but it fell flat.

Chelle grabbed their purses, handed Joey hers and opened the bathroom door. When they stepped out, Dante was leaning up against the wall. The sight of him startled Joey because she didn't know he was at the party, much less in the country. He was in Africa for another two weeks the last she'd heard.

"Hey," he said when she was obviously too taken aback to speak. "I thought I'd surprise you."

"Oh. Well, I'm surprised," Joey huffed. "When did you get here?"

"I've been here since the owner's speech. I came straight from the airport."

Chelle couldn't even hide the dismay on her face when the realization set in that Dante most likely heard Joey and Shane's little spat. Joey had a stunned expression in her eyes, but she still managed an uncertain smile.

"We were just about to leave," she stammered.

"So soon?" Dante's feigned surprise was too much for Chelle, who turned her head.

"Yeah. I'm going back to the hotel with Chelle. To talk."

Dante nodded, standing up straight to step forward and swipe an errant tear from the corner of Joey's eyes.

"Coming home tonight?"

"No. I have a room. I had planned –"

"I'll be out of the apartment by the time you get back.

Joey gasped at the implication of his words but didn't reply. What could she even say? The last time they'd seen each other was Chelle's wedding, where he'd had the altercation with Shane, and now she was certain he'd overheard her outburst. What could she do?

Their relationship had become collateral damage to the Joey and Shane show, or more like a shit show.

"Dante," Joey sighed. She wasn't sure what to say, but she knew he deserved better than their current situation. "We should talk."

"I was hoping we could do that, but it looks like it's too late. I wasn't sure before. You know? I had my suspicions, but I asked you, and you always said he was just a friend. Your number one client. But at the wedding, I knew there was more to it." He let his words trail off because it was apparent what came next. They were standing in the aftermath of it.

Nodding to Chelle and then Remy, who had just joined them, Dante pushed his hands in his pockets and walked off. The tears returned to Joey's eyes, full force, as she watched him walk away. Even though she didn't want what he wanted, she felt terrible that she hurt him.

"I think you guys can talk tomorrow once everyone has calmed down," Chelle suggested.

"What's going on? Shane just damn near dragged Kelly outside to talk."

"It's a long story," Chelle replied. "But let's go out whatever door they didn't."

Chapter 10

After Chelle left, Joey thought she felt better. She poured herself one last glass of wine and sat on the couch, trying to relax. But her mood plummeted when she looked around the luxurious hotel suite and remembered why she was there, and that Shane wasn't with her. It felt like something inside her had snapped into jagged pieces that were piercing her heart. Just when she finally allowed herself to believe she could have it all, it was all ripped away.

When she eventually checked her phone, she wasn't surprised to see that Shane had called several times. As much as she was upset with him, she also kept replaying the horrified expression on his face when he burst into the restroom and saw her in such a troubled state. She knew he wouldn't hurt her on purpose, but hurt was hurt, and she felt it.

The following day, she got dressed and headed to the dance studio. On the weekends and one night a week, she taught two dance classes for young girls: one hip-hop jazz class for ages 8-12 and one cheer prep class for ages 12-18. She'd been teaching since she moved to L.A. and finally found a schedule that worked for her. Dancing had always been her first love, and she found a way to continue her passion.

Tiffany, her assistant instructor who would step in if Joey was busy, sick or couldn't make a class for any reason, asked her if she was okay the minute she stepped into the dance studio. Joey assured her she was fine and then proceeded to leave it all on the floor. She took it easy on the younger girls, but the teens got an intense practice, which they seemed to love because they kept up with her pace.

Afterward, she stayed behind, using the time to tweak a few new routines she planned on implementing. Tiffany worked with her for a while and then left when she sensed that Joey wanted her alone time, which she did. Joey liked to lose herself in the music and let it guide the movement of her body. Every so often, the pain would be so much that she pushed herself too hard and wound up missing a step or winded. She was on the floor trying to catch her breath after pushing herself too hard. Looking back, she realized Shane was leaning against the door, watching her.

When he saw that she noticed him, he stepped closer toward her.

"I had to see how you were." His voice was laden with remorse.
"I'll live," she replied scathingly.
"I didn't sleep last night worrying about you."
"I guess I should feel honored by that?"
"Joey."

"Shane. I don't know what you want from me. I would have returned your phone calls if I was ready to talk to you. I don't know if I'll ever be ready."

She felt the tears burning the corners of her eyes and turned her back on him. Crying in front of Shane was the last thing she wanted to do. Not because he'd never seen her cry before, but because she didn't want him to know just how much he ruined her. How much he'd broken her heart.

Joey heard Shane's footsteps behind her and wasn't surprised when she felt his hand on her shoulder. He then slipped both hands under her arms to lift her up. Joey wanted to push him away, but the sad part was that she needed the hug that only he could give her. Shane had been her champion, comforter, and protector for so long, it was inconceivable that he'd be the one she needed consoling from.

She let him hold her for a moment, reveling in his scent and strong embrace before she attempted to pull away.

"Joey, sorry is too lame to say, but just know I would never hurt you."

She knew those words were supposed to make her feel better, but they just exacerbated her hurt.

"And what am I supposed to do with that, Shane? Is that gonna put my heart back together? Is it going to erase the last twenty-four hours and put us back to a time when we had a future together, and you weren't having a baby with someone else?" Her shouts reverberated off the mirrored walls of the large room as they faced off.

"Joey, it's not true. And I'm not just saying that."
"Did you fuck her?"
"What do you mean?"
"Did you fuck her?" She yelled. "Did you insert your penis into her vagina and ejaculate inside her? Is there a scientific possibility that she could actually be pregnant with your baby?"

His silence was answer enough. Joey shoved him out of anger and frustration when he couldn't assure her there was nothing to worry about. She spun away from him, scared that she would do more than just push him if she didn't move away.

"I did sleep with her. Months ago, but I used protection like I always do. I pulled out and came in the condom, which I flushed. You know I'm not reckless."
"I've seen you very reckless," she scoffed.
"With you," he corrected. "Only with you."

Joey let out a pent-up scream of rage. She was incensed because it was Kelly, and Shane had spent so much time trying to convince her that his ex meant nothing. He had women all across the world lined up to sleep with him, but the one he told her not to worry about was now carrying his child. She almost wished it was a stranger. Joey kept moving until she was at the wall, leaning against the dance bar as she looked at his reflection over her shoulder. She saw him approaching her and turned with her hands out to halt his progress.

"All these years, you blew me off whenever I brought her up. She's boring. She's just a friend. You don't see her in that way."

"Don't do that to me, Joey. Don't make me out to be some mindless man-child who can't control his dick. I fucked my ex, who I've known for over ten years, that I thought I could trust. What she's doing now has nothing to do with sex and everything to do with money. I've already requested the paternity test, and Chelle is working up a cease-and-desist letter to keep her from talking about me or the baby until we clear all this up.

"Please, Shane. Just give me time."

"This is killing me, too," he shouted. "I hate to see you hurting like this because of me, and I hate that she's lying. I know that baby isn't mine, Joey. And I know that doesn't mean anything to you right now. But I'll prove it, and I'll be the one to put your heart back together."

He grabbed her hand and kissed it, unable to be that close to her and not touch her in some way. Unable to leave without somehow feeling her one last time. Joey watched him walk out, and her heart began to ache all over again. She sunk to the ground, her head falling between her knees. For the first time, she really grasped the concept of what life would be like without Shane, and she felt like she couldn't breathe. She hoped with everything in her that he was right, but until she knew for sure, she had to act accordingly.

Her relationship with Dante had already suffered; she wasn't going to fuck up her career too.

Joey and Shane hard-launching their relationship while his long-term ex-girlfriend was carrying his child would be career suicide for her. No amount of spinning or good press would clean that up, and if she didn't lose the clients she had, it would hinder new business. Nobody wants a messy publicist.

∞

That Monday morning, she walked into the office on a mission. The first order of business was to reorganize her workload. Joey wasn't a workaholic like Chelle, who would bury herself in projects to cover up her pain. She needed to take time off to decompress. Their five-year college reunion was coming up, and she needed her mind right if she was going to be able to be around Shane. She also wanted to get back in shape and added a few workouts to her schedule.

Delegating her simple tasks and "easy" clients to her assistant, she also shifted Shane to her boss, Stew. She knew he'd been dying to work with Shane up close and personal, and he was the only person she could trust to do what needed to be done and not let it get to his head. When she requested the change, Stew's eyebrows went sky-high. He played it off but insisted she be a part of the meeting with Shane and Chelle to discuss handling the media buzz about Kelly's pregnancy.

The look on Shane's face when Stew announced he would be handling his file for a few months hit Joey like a sucker punch. It was a slight reaction, imperceptible to the others in the room. He clenched his jaw and refused to look at her. Eye contact and reading each other's moods was part of what made their relationship what it was. Just like she couldn't let him see her crying, he wouldn't want her to see the hurt in his eyes.

After the introductions, Joey excused herself. Chelle was stunned by her actions but had the presence of mind to put a hand on Shane's arm to keep him from following Joey out of the conference room. Back in her office, Joey gathered her purse and jacket and headed home. Not only did she want to avoid Shane, but she wasn't ready to face Dante either. She hadn't been home since the party and wasn't prepared to deal with him at the office.

The office was the only place she wasn't her usual bubbly self. She strived to project an air of confidence and competence, so feeling the way she did was a liability. Meaning, that she was liable to snap on the first person who tried her, which often happened in an industry where everyone wanted to be the top dog. Her connections to Shane, Dom, and Jay, along with a slew of their associates and friends, put her in a hard spot to reach. Having that many powerhouse clients under her belt at such a young age made her a target everyone was trying to reach.

Joey sauntered out of the office as quickly as she could without looking like she was running. She sent out a few emails from her E-Class Mercedes Coupe, and then drove out of the office parking garage. The ride from downtown to her apartment in Fairfax was short since there was no traffic at that time of the day. She was able to grab lunch from her favorite Thai restaurant and a few extra bottles of her favorite wine.

Inside her apartment, it further reminded her that her life was in upheaval. Dante had moved, just like he said he would, and while he left most of the essential furniture and appliances, his personal touches like trophies, awards, and family pictures were gone. The pictures of them as a couple, however, were still there. Joey sighed as she explored the penthouse apartment, confirming that he'd wiped his presence from her life.

She changed into her FAMU sweats before returning to the kitchen to plate her food and pour a generous glass of wine. One of Chelle's playlists helped to drown out her thoughts while she fought to keep her mood from plummeting into the pits of hell. She was twirling a forkful of Pad Thai noodles when Dante walked in the door, staring like he caught her after a long search. There was no missing the accusatory glint to his expression, and Joey braced herself for what came next.

"Your assistant said you'd gone home for the day and took the rest of the week off?"
Joey put down her fork with a sigh. "Yeah. I have some personal shit to take care of, and I need to clear my head."
"Some personal shit? Now you talkin' to me like I'm just a coworker." He tossed his keys on the kitchen island and loosened his tie.

"It's the answer I would give anyone right now," she replied.
"Anyone? I'm not just anyone. What the fuck, Joey? I told you I'm moving out after I overheard... Shit, I don't even know what the fuck that was. And you don't think I deserve a

conversation? We've been together for three years!"

"I'm fucked up right now, Dante. I fucked up with you, and for that, I do want to apologize. I should have been honest with you sooner."

"Honest with me sooner about the fact that you're in love with Shane Duncan? Is that how we finish that sentence? Was he always the endgame, and was I just a placeholder?"

"No. I got with you because I care about you and stayed because I love you. My relationship with Shane was complicated, and one day, it wasn't anymore."

"So, while you were with me, you figured out that you wanted to be with your 'best friend' from college. This just keeps getting worse. You know, when they said you were out, a part of me was hoping that it was because you regretted losing me. The stupid part of me, I guess. The delusional part that refused to accept what my intuition was telling me. What my eyes were telling me. I chose to trust your words instead."

"You're not being fair. First of all, the open relationship was something we both agreed to, and don't think I didn't know about Jennifer. You dated her for almost the entire first year we were together. Open means open. You always run the risk of the other person meeting someone else."

"That is true, but I wasn't in love with Jennifer. I just enjoyed her company. You lied about your feelings for Shane."

"I never lied. You asked me if I love him, and I said yes. I just never considered him as someone I could be with. We weren't sleeping with each other, and he was doing his thing in the NBA..."

"So, what changed? Huh?"

Dante's rhetorical question hung between them when she had no answer. How did she explain that missing Shane like crazy and having a secret meet-up in Italy is what changed everything?

"Let me guess," he continued. "You wound up fucking him, and he gassed you up like these ballers do to think you guys were gonna be together. Now you find out he's having a baby with his real girlfriend."

Joey turned away from him to look out at their view of the city. There was a time when she loved coming home to that apartment and coming home to Dante. Then, the phone calls from Shane became more frequent, the video calls increased, and soon, she was flying out to see him at his away games, where they'd hide out in the hotel together.

Dante's brutal interpretation of events caused unexpected tears to spring into Joey's eyes. Hearing it from someone else's vantage point made her feel sick inside. Especially when he made her sound so stupid. She knew it wasn't that simple. Or was it?

"I guess I deserve that," she mumbled.

Letting out a heavy sigh, Dante joined her at the floor-to-ceiling window that used to symbolize the city where they planned to build their empire together. He only wished it was as simple as finding out that Joey slept with Shane, but hearing her scream in such agony, he knew her feelings were deeper. Even if she somehow decided to stay with him, her feelings for Shane would always be between them.

"I shouldn't have said that," he said, touching her lower back.
"It might be the truth."
"We both know it's not. I've seen the way that man looks at you. The way you look at each other. I'm sure you'll overcome whatever is happening now. I was selfish to stay. I guess this was my payback because Jennifer was in love with me."
"Probably still is if you listen to gossip," Joey replied.

She turned around to face him, unable to stop the tears that came. It was a bittersweet moment because she knew he loved her more than she loved him, but that would never be enough.

"I wish things could be different," she sniffed.

Dante rubbed a finger under her chin, swiping at a tear that had slid down her cheeks. "Me too."

He hugged her before grabbing his keychain and removing the two keys and fob that gave him access to their apartment and building. With one last look around the apartment, he walked out.

Chapter 11

The wedding party had just returned to the hotel after Kiko and Dom's joint bachelor/bachelorette party. Everyone gathered in the lobby, still hopped up on the excitement of the night. Some people chose to go to bed, others headed for the beach, and Shane and a couple of the guys congregated at the bar. Joey and Kiko's cousins were dancing to old-school reggae until Dante pulled her aside to talk.

"So, I'm trying to get to know your pretty ass, for real," he whispered against her ear. They had been flirting all night, and after Shane's lap dance, Dante felt he needed to up his game.

"What do you wanna know?" Joey toyed with the buttons on his shirt as they talked, her playful, flirtatious vibe in full effect. It was her nature, even if it was just in fun.

"Everythang."

Joey gave Dante a long once-over. He was tall, not NBA tall, but he had a good three inches on her. His smooth brown skin was supple and blemish free, and he had the kindest smile.

While there was something about Dante that she liked, Joey found herself glancing over his shoulder at Shane. He'd been watching them initially but then turned his attention to Kiko's cousin, who had been gushing all over him since she arrived on the island. Joey almost forgot some of her friends were stars until she witnessed how certain people acted around them. Even though she had no right to be upset, it pissed her off every time she saw Shane giving China so much attention.

"I think I'm heading to bed. Wanna walk me to my room?" She nodded toward the exit, indicating that she was ready to leave.

"I would love, too," Dante replied without hesitation.

He grabbed Joey's hand, and she followed him out of the bar. She glanced back to catch Shane glaring at them even though China was practically in his lap. Cutting her eyes, she focused back on Dante. He was the kind of man she claimed was her type. A businessman in the same industry, which was a plus, was good-looking, athletic, and had a master plan. From their few conversations, they aligned with their goals, and he appreciated her ambition, even suggesting ways he could assist her in getting to the next level.

Chemistry-wise, she'd given him a seven out of ten. She was attracted to him, but not to the point where it affected her thinking. No, he didn't sweep her off her feet, but that wasn't what she was looking for. Joey wanted something planted firmly in reality. Her grandmother's words were never far from the forefront of her mind, and she wasn't going to let any man throw her off her focus.

When they reached her room, she leaned her back against the door, and Dante placed his hand above her head, leaning in.

"So. I guess this is goodnight." Joey placed a hand on his broad chest to feel his heart beating.

"It doesn't have to be." He dipped his head, and she raised her face to meet him halfway. His lips were soft as they melded to hers, surprising her. She placed her hand behind his head as she returned the kiss and added a little heat to it by tracing his lips with her tongue.

"Wow," he whispered when she pulled away. The kiss was sweet and steamy, and Joey smiled up at him through lowered lashes. Before she could reply, her phone dinged with a message, and she angled her screen away from his view.

Stalk: Get rid of him

Joey gulped down her gasp, pretending to yawn. She put her phone away as if the text was insignificant. Part of her wanted to ignore Shane. Who was he to order her around like that? But she wasn't sure what to expect from him and didn't want to cause any drama. He wasn't the same boy she met in freshman year of college, and while they'd always pulled rank over others, he had never been so direct. She hated that her panties were soaking wet because of it.

"Well, it's late, and I've got a big day ahead of me tomorrow. I should probably get some sleep. Save me a dance tomorrow?"

"Sure will," Dante replied with his hand over his heart. He kissed her once more before watching her open her door and wave goodnight. If he was disappointed, he didn't let it show.

Joey closed her room door and vacillated between calling Shane to curse him out and being turned on by his apparent jealousy. Not sure if he would call or show up, she ran to the bathroom to brush her teeth and gargle with mouthwash. She heard a knock at her door as soon as she turned off the faucet. She checked her hair in the mirror before heading to the door to let Shane in. When she opened it, she faked an attitude, prepped to give him a hard time for acting so possessive.

"Can I help you?"

Instead of answering, he rolled his eyes and hoisted her off her feet, carrying her into the room and kicking the door closed. When he put her down, she shoved him, and he grabbed her arms, pulling her against him.

"Don't you know how to ask? You don't own me, Shane!"

"Quit being dramatic. Did you want the entire world to know that I'm coming to your room at two in the morning?" Kicking off his shoes, he walked to the bathroom to wash his hands and face.

"What if I hadn't planned on letting you in?" She asked from behind him as he leaned over the sink. "What if I had company?"

Shane stood there, slightly stumped by her question, as if it hadn't dawned on him that she wouldn't let him in. Joey shook her head and returned to the room, leaving him to ponder. Then he thought about the fact that she got rid of Dante as he requested, and he'd caught a faint whiff of Listerine when he walked past her. His expression changed to a smug grin as he followed after her.

"So, you don't want to see me?"

"That's not the point."

"It's absolutely the point," he said, grabbing her hand and pulling her closer. "I can't believe you kissed him."

Before she could tell him it was none of his business, he dipped his head to look straight into her eyes. Playing stubborn, even though she was getting more aroused by the second, Joey turned her head away, and gave him her cheek. Shane's chuckle rumbled against her ears, and it vibrated down her spine to contribute to the fire radiating from her core. Instead of pushing him away, her fingers flexed with the need to clutch him closer.

Visions of their past encounters flickered through her mind. Her skin was sensitive and tight, and when he licked from behind her ear to her collarbone, she trembled.

Shane continued to tease her by placing soft kisses along the side of her face and breathing deep, husky moans against her ear. Joey panted with unbridled desire, fighting to stifle her moans as she carried on with her fake rejection. His fingers toyed with the zipper at the front of her dress that would open her up from the top down. Her fingers covered his as if she were trying to halt his progress, but when he began to pull, she barely exerted any pressure to stop him.

"You don't own me." She echoed her earlier sentiment. "You don't get to tell me what to do. I can't believe you had the nerve to tell me to get rid of him."

"I can't tell you what to do?" Shane nipped at her ear. "I see you got rid of him, though."

Joey exhaled a deep breath to mask her whimper. "I have to wake up early."

"You ain't gettin' no sleep tonight."

Shane's words were a sultry whisper against her neck as he fully unzipped her dress and pushed it open, revealing a provocative, delicate, lace lingerie set that barely concealed the dark shape of her areola and the V shape of her mound. He groaned at the visual loveliness. Leaning down, he sucked the puckered tip of her nipple onto his tongue, lashing it before scoring it with his teeth. Unable to hold back any longer, Joey cried out as her pleasure mingled with the sting of pain.

"Get on the bed, on your hands and knees," he instructed.

They stared deep into each other's eyes, lust and all types of sordid desires emanating between them. This was Shane's way of proving that he *could* and would tell her what to do, and Joey didn't hesitate to listen. They both knew that she would do whatever he told her, and that knowledge was what always got them into trouble. The boundaries they created for each other were just for show and were often crossed and blurred because of their feelings. The illicit pleasure they derived from giving in to each other was their own brand of addictive drug.

Joey backed away from him slowly and then turned and crawled onto the bed. She positioned herself on her hands and knees, revealing that her panties were also crotchless. Looking over her shoulder, she caught the slight hiss he released as he bit the corner of his lip when he noticed. They shared a look of complicity to each other's desires. His eyes darkened as he approached her, and her spine quivered as she quaked with anticipation.

"You look so fuckin' good. Turn around and stay facing that way." His deep voice broke the silence. "I can see your pussy glistening for me already. Tell me why you're so wet, baby." He teased her ass cheeks with a light slap to each one.

"I don't know," she moaned in response.

"I don't believe that. Something or someone has you dripping like this."

Two fingers crept up her leg, from her calf to her thigh and then slowed as it neared her entrance. Shane grinned as Joey wiggled her ass, expecting that he would slide them inside of her. Instead, he slid his fingers up and around to caress her lower back. She groaned in agony.

"It's you," she cried.

"Me? You sure it's not from that little kiss outside your door?" He peppered her cheeks with a few more slaps that grew firmer each time. Then he gripped and massaged a cheek.

"No," she moaned. "Not him. You."

"What about me?"

He took his hand off her, stepping back to remove his clothing. Joey felt the loss of his presence but heard the rustling and knew what he was doing. Her breathing deepened as she fought the urge to touch herself. Shane knew how to tease her just right because he knew how much she relished the buildup. When he was naked, he grabbed her ankles, spreading her legs a little further apart.

"Look at my juicy pussy." He blew over her sensitive spot, then bit her inner thigh.

"Ahh," Joey yelped at the unexpected sting of his bite. Her head fell forward while she awaited his next move.

"I had you that wet before I even touched you? Why?" His hands glided up her legs, stopping at her thigh.

"Because you turn me on."

"What about me turns you on?"

"Shane!"

"Answer me." He bit her thigh again.

"The way you look at me," she panted.

"What else?"

"The way you touch me."

"How do I touch you?"

"You just always know what to do to me."

"Cause I always know what you need. Like right now."

He leaned forward, pulling her backward until her pussy was grazing his lips. Flicking his tongue out, he placed it flat against her until the tip brushed against her clit. Then, he began to lick her with long, deliberate strokes until she was trembling under his touch. When he pushed his tongue inside of her, she cried out.

"Oh my God, that feels so good." Her fingers clutched the comforter as she bore down on him.

"You taste so good," he murmured.

"Keep doing that with your tongue," she panted. "Don't stop!"

"Mhm," he hummed, sending shockwaves to her core.

Joey mewled and whimpered as her climax erupted. Her back arched deeper as she chased the thrust of his tongue. His firm and consistent pressure was exquisite, and when he reached a hand underneath her to squeeze her clit, the dam burst. Literally. She released a deep, throaty groan as a stream of her essence coated his tongue. His satisfied moans had her clenching for more.

"I need to be inside you."

Shane rose behind her and eased her back down to deepen her arch. Grabbing a gold foil packet, he quickly sheathed himself before lining the head of his dick to her entrance. Still reeling from her orgasm, her slick canal was still clenching in ecstasy. With a slow thrust, he slid the tip in and then right back out, loving the way she was dripping around him.

"Ooh," Joey groaned in frustration. Her fingers dug into the mattress when he did it again. "Shane!"

Her deep growl was followed by her raring back on him until he was almost completely inside her. With a pump of his hips, he pushed into her as deep as he could go. They both moaned wildly as he filled her to the hilt and then pulled out to the tip. He repeated the motion, increasing in speed and intensity until he was blowing her back all the way out. Joey's cries and moans spurred him on as he fought not to lose it.

"I feel you, baby. I feel that pussy squeezing the shit out my dick. Let it go, babe." He smacked each cheek a few times to punctuate his command, and her body lurched forward as she orgasmed again. Following her motion, Shane leaned forward until his entire body hovered over her and began rolling his pelvis, hitting her with slow, deep strokes as he kissed her neck and ears. Her body convulsed and shook as he fucked her through her climax.

"Fuck," he shouted as his hips bucked with the need to release. "You're trying to take me down, but I'm not done with you yet."

Joey squeaked into her pillow, clenching the sheets in her fist as he worked her over. She cried out when he bit into her shoulder, gripping her hips and encouraging her to fuck him back.

"Come on, baby, give it to me. Don't hold back. I wanna feel you creaming all over me again."

"Shit, Shane!" Joey threw it back on him until they synced their pace. The sounds of their grunts, groans, and skin slapping against skin filled the room until she released a hoarse scream into the pillow as another climax began to overtake her.

"That's it," he growled against her shoulder. His teeth latched onto her soft skin, and she shuddered as her essence flooded his shaft. "Fuck, Joey. That pussy drowning me!"

"You do this to me," she groaned hoarsely.

Shane slowed down his stroke, rearing back on his knees to look down on her. He kneaded and massaged her lower back and cheeks to relax her even more.

"I missed you," he moaned. "You're the only one that makes me feel like I can fuck all night."

"Mmm," was all she could manage; she felt like he was lulling her into another realm.

Slowly, he pulled out and rolled onto his back. "Come ride me, baby."

Somehow, Joey mustered up the strength to clamber on top of him. Bracing herself with her hands on his shoulders, she let him guide his shaft inside of her. His resulting groan caused a ripple of desire down her back. She began to rock back and forth, matching the slow pace he set when he was behind her.

Shane closed his eyes as he enjoyed the feel of Joey's slippery walls contracting around him as her hips danced in a circular motion. His hands groped and massaged her ass cheeks, spreading them so that her juices were dripping onto him. His fingers edged to the spot where their bodies came together, and he swirled her essence down toward her backdoor. She was so wet; he didn't need any lubricant to slip his middle finger inside her tight hole.

Joey released a sequence of guttural exclamations at the unexpected pleasure. She swayed forward while his other hand pressed down on her back, and he arched upwards. He began to ease his finger in and out at a slow, measured pace. The exquisite sensation of feeling full back there had Joey close to the edge. She bounced on him as he matched her with upward thrusts, the pressure from his finger causing her to cry out his name as she detonated again.

"Oh God," she whimpered until his mouth swallowed all her sex noises.

Their kiss was feverish and desperate—Joey's with ecstasy and his with the pent-up need to release. Shane relished in her tidal wave and the way she constricted around his length. As her body continued to shudder with her release, he pulled out and repositioned himself until the head of his dick was pressing against her tight bud. They had done it before and loved it, and he knew this position was easiest for her because she could work her way down his shaft at her pace.

When Shane was fully seated inside her, he rolled over, placing her on her back. He moaned in delicious agony because he knew he wouldn't last long. Pulling out slowly, inch by inch, he took his time pushing back in, careful not to hurt her. Joey's fingers dug into his back as she trembled from the intense pressure and fullness of him. Every thrust was rewarded with a tortured cry as she pressed her face into his chest to muffle her screams of passion.

"Fuck, Joey," he gritted between his teeth.
"Shane," she hissed. "Fuck me, please."
"You ready?"
"Please!"
Her head fell to the side, and Shane nuzzled his face into her neck, inching in and out of her until his name was a perpetual prayer from her lips. Sliding his arms underneath her, he scooped her into his embrace, cradling her close. The slow winding motion of his hips brought them both to the edge and then he'd stop, kissing her to quell her pleas for him to let her come.

"That feel good, baby?"
"Mmm," she moaned deeply.

His dick pulsed inside her as it expanded and hardened in preparation for his release. "You feel that? I'm gonna come so hard," he grunted.

"I feel it," she whimpered.

"You want it harder?"

"Yes!"

Giving her what she needed, his hips snapped as he pumped her harder. Shane couldn't hold in the loud groans and shouts that slipped from his mouth as he succumbed to the intensity of his climax. Joey sobbed his name until she was hoarse, her orgasm crashing at the sounds of his ecstasy.

"Oh! Fuck me," Shane's voice boomed as he exploded inside of her, the snug fit allowing her to feel every spasm and jerk of his dick until he crumpled on top of her.

"Fuck," he panted as he kissed the side of her face, unable to think or move.

Joey entwined her fingers in his wild afro and massaged his scalp and neck. Shane pressed his forehead into her shoulder as he fought to catch his breath. His body still grinding into her on impulse. She felt his erection stirring again and couldn't believe it.

"I don't want to pull out," he murmured against her skin with a kiss. "But I gotta change this condom."

"Change?" Joey's skeptical whisper hung between them as he cautiously slid out.

"I said you wasn't getting any sleep tonight. You wanna keep this from me for years? I've got some making up to do."

∞

The next day was Kiko's wedding, and after being woken up in the morning to Shane's head sliding between her legs, she was dragging her ass in the bridal suite.

"As my mother would say, you look like you been rode hard and put away wet," Chelle whispered in her ear.

"Both," Joey replied. She was struggling to put on her jewelry, so Chelle took over.

"Let me guess. Dante?"

Joey thought for a moment before answering the question. The night they had didn't erase the conversation where they both agreed that they were not each other's type when it came to settling down. What would be the point in telling Chelle that Shane had rocked her world when that would only lead to more discourse on them getting together? On the other hand, she did have plans to see where things would lead with Dante. So, she lied.

She hated not being able to gush about Shane, but sometimes, it was just easier to keep him a secret.

Chapter 12

It had been three days since Dante left, and aside from her classes at the dance studio, Joey hadn't left her apartment. There were so many things that she'd taken for granted, just living in the moment, that when they were gone, it hit hard. The breakup with Dante was hitting her much harder than she expected. Three years of them being together reduced to a few pictures scattered around her apartment. The friendship and intimacy that she'd come to rely on, over and done.

Not speaking to Shane every day or being able to call him to talk about how she was feeling was also tough. Besides Chelle, he was the one she could vent to who would just listen. If she asked him for advice, he would drop a few gems on her, but for the most part, he'd always been her shoulder to cry on. As the days passed and her anger subsided, she wondered what their path would be.

Joey was packing up some items that Dante left behind and changing up the decor of her place. A fresh start was in order, and she even considered breaking her lease to truly have a new beginning. She was taking down a painting that Dante had bought for the living room when her intercom buzzed. Not sure who it could be, she checked her phone for missed calls or messages before hitting the call button.

"Hello?"

"It's your fairy Godmothers. Let us up!"

"Who?" Joey giggled, clearly recognizing Nicole's voice.

"Bitch! Push the buzzer," Chelle yelled back.

Joey laughed as she went to the front door to let her friends in. When she opened it to find Kiko with them, and that they'd brought their babies, she burst into tears.

"Oh, honey bun," Chelle consoled her as she pulled her into a hug.

"Jojo!" Kiko's little boy, Dommy, called out to her as J.J., Nicole's baby, was wiggling with a two-tooth smile in his mother's arms, so Joey took him, and he snuggled right up to her. His little body fitting perfectly in her embrace caused the tears to flow harder. Kiko completed the group hug, picking up her toddler, who was also reaching for his godbrother. The group broke apart, and Joey took J.J. and sat on the couch where Dommy clamored to sit on her lap.

Joey felt overwhelmed with the love and support and tried to hide her face in J.J.'s chest as she cried. She felt hands rubbing her shoulders and back as the girls consoled her.

"It's gonna be ok, bookie," Chelle cooed.

"We're here now, honey. What's going on?" Kiko plopped down on the shag rug at Joey's feet.

"Let me enjoy my babies for a little bit before we take the plunge," Joey murmured as she nuzzled J.J. for his baby scent. At seven months old, he was the cutest mixture of Jay and Nicole. Dommy was the spitting image of his daddy except with Kiko's eyes.

For a while, the girls made small talk about babies and their upcoming five-year reunion. As expected, they planned for the whole group to meet up and attend the party together. They would need a big house to accommodate the new little additions to their found family. Everything was planned down to which parents would be commissioned for childcare to needing a house with a mother-in-law suite.

Eventually both babies went down for a nap, Kiko had an early dinner delivered, and the wine was flowing. Joey's spirits had been lifted so much that she dreaded even having the conversation about what was wrong. She tried to keep the mood upbeat, but Kiko wasn't having it.

"Ok. I done flown across the country. Someone's gonna tell me what's up." She leaned back, waiting for Joey to start talking.

"You flew across the country because Dom had a meeting out here," Joey replied.

"Actually, I hadn't planned on coming, so my ass is here for you,"

"Oh," Joey said meekly as she sank lower in her seat.

"Well, something is up. Shane ain't picking up his phone, and you been missing from the group chat all week," Nicole surmised.

"I didn't want to spill your tea," Chelle chimed in.

Joey released a sigh. "I feel good now. Don't make me ruin it."

"It's gonna be ruined the moment we leave, so you might as well let it out," Chelle countered.

"Dante stopped by on Monday to make our breakup official," she said.

"And why are you and Dante breaking up?" Kiko's tone was inquisitive and tinged with annoyance. "And please keep in mind that some of us don't know all the sordid details."

"Long story short?"

"Nope. Long story long!" Kiko dragged out her words for emphasis. Nicole and Chelle laughed while Joey shook her head.

"It is what it is," Joey shrugged in frustration. "Yes, I always liked Shane. Yes, y'all have already deduced that we've been messing around. But–"

"Ooh, honesty! Yes," Kiko cheered.

"Can I finish, or?" Joey just glared at her.

"Sorry. Please, continue," Kiko replied.

"Dante and I had an open relationship. I wasn't ready to settle down and he was still dating a girl named Jennifer. I should have known what it was because I wasn't even really upset about it. I wanted to do my thing, and our schedules sucked, so instead of breaking up, I suggested we just be open."

There was a collective murmur of responses from the girls, and Joey paused for effect. Kiko waved her on to continue while Chelle poured more wine.

"By this point, Shane and I are spending more time together. I'm going to more games; he's flying me out to meet him. Calling–"

"Flying you out to Italy," Nicole chimed in.

"Calling me all the time," Joey continued, ignoring Nicole's outburst. "Dante was traveling, and Shane was pressing me. Shane's dumb ass signed a contract with Kelly to clean up his image in Phoenix so he could get that two-year extension deal. So, we had to keep things under wraps because being out in the open would hurt his reputation and kill my career."

"Yeah, you wouldn't be winning publicist of the year with that scandal," Nicole agreed.

"Right," Joey sighed. "I know it was selfish, but I didn't break up with Dante because part of me wasn't sure if things would pan out with Shane. He'd been doing all that partying and shit. We met up in Italy last year, and he promised that we would make things official as soon as the contract expired in a month or so. We got him signed to LA, so he couldn't care less about his image now, but there's still the little issue of my career. Well, last week at his signing party, Kelly announced that she was pregnant."

"Damn," Nicole gasped. "I hoped that was just a rumor."

Kiko just shook her head.

"But we're still not sure it's his," Chelle added.

"Well, he stopped by the dance studio over the weekend. He says he's getting a paternity test, but he can't deny that he slept with her," Joey replied.

"And him leaving a pregnant girlfriend is messy as fuck," Kiko added.

"Exactly," Joey sighed.

"Damn," Nicole exclaimed. "That bitch knew her time was up and was trying to keep him with a baby?"

"She knows he doesn't want her for real. This is about money and one-upping me." Joey threw herself back against the cushions, pissed off all over again.

"That heifer!" Kiko kissed her teeth, sounding just like her grandmother. "Everybody knows that babies can't keep a man. He'll be gone in less than a year!"

"See, I don't think so," Joey countered. "Shane has had this weird ass thing with Kelly for years. He might just settle with her for the baby's sake because of how he grew up. He's adamant that he wants his children to have both parents."

"Girl. You crazy as hell if you think Shane is gonna let this keep him from being with you," Chelle said.

"You've been beating us over the head with that 'just a friend' BS for years, but it doesn't mean we believe it. That man is in love with you." Nicole folded her arms across her chest and shook her head.

"Y'all don't understand," Joey sighed. "Family is very important to him."

"I get that," Chelle agreed. "But he has the resources to ensure that his child goes without nothing, and the heart to make sure he does whatever it takes to be the best father he can be."

"You think so?"

"I know so," Kiko affirmed.

"Joey? What do you want?" Nicole leaned forward to ask her questions. "Do you want to be with Shane?"

"Yes," she said with a sad sigh.

"Amen," Kiko shouted.

"And Hallelujah!" Nicole threw a praise hand in the air.

Chelle chuckled as the girls celebrated Joey finally being honest about her feelings. "It is so refreshing to get a straight answer out of you. God knows."

"Well, there's no point hiding it anymore," Joey smirked.

"So, what happened to Dante? Was it because of the skirmish at the wedding?" Nicole inquired.

"Sort of. He was pissed about that, but he snuck into Shane's signing party and overheard me and Shane –"

"Your lover's quarrel," Chelle chimed in.

"Wait. He came back from Africa to surprise you? Or was he trying to catch you out there? Because it makes no sense that you didn't know he was back in the country." Nicole stated.

"Good point. I guess it doesn't really matter. He heard my crying. Heard Shane pleading with me. Telling me he loved me. It wasn't hard to fill in the blanks."

"I'm lost," Nicole said. "Did you ever really want to be with Dante? Because why be in an open relationship?"

"Dante had everything I was looking for, on paper, but I wasn't ready to settle down at first. It wasn't until Chelle's wedding that he brought up being exclusive, but I think that was because of Shane."

"On paper? Girl, this is real life, and you ain't marrying a stick figure. You didn't want that man. Just admit it!" Kiko shook her head and sipped her wine

"I knew what I wanted."

"Yes. We all know about your list," Chelle said with air quotes. "But life doesn't work that way. Your list doesn't take your heart and feelings into consideration."

"So now what, boo bear?"' Nicole asked while rubbing Joey's shoulders.

"It's bookie," Joey laughed at her attempt to be comforting. "You are getting better, though."

"Hey! What if I prefer boo bear?"

"Then I'll be your boo bear." Joey leaned into her for a hug.

Kiko patted Joey's thigh. "Ok, boo bear. What happens next?"

"She needs to talk to Shane. I mean, let's be real. Y'all were both being messy, so you can't be too mad at him for getting caught up. You could have gotten pregnant by Dante."

"We use protection," Joey replied dryly.

"Every time? For three years?" Kiko grimaced.

"Well, thank God we don't have to worry about that, but Shane didn't really do anything wrong," Nicole said, side-eyeing Kiko for her last comment.

"Right," Chelle agreed with Nicole's assessment. "And you know he needs his friend. He didn't speak again after you passed him off to Stew and left the meeting. I've never seen him like this before, and I don't like it."

Joey hung her head. "I told him I need some time. I allowed myself to really dream, you know? And it's all falling apart. Things are over before we even started."

Chelle squeezed her arm in understanding. "It doesn't have to be over. It just won't be as easy as you imagined. But life never is."

"Let's rewind for a bit," Kiko said after a sip of wine. "I want to revisit the Dante situation."

"Must we? I already feel horrible enough about it." Joey sipped her drink.

"But that's what I want to examine. You say you love him. What if he's a better option for you?"

Chelle and Nicole exchanged a befuddled glance while waiting for Joey's answer.

"Are you feeling ok? I think you may have missed the part where Dante broke up with me and moved out," Joey said, gesturing around the apartment.

Kiko waved her off. "Please, you can get him back if you really want to. But, what if Kelly's baby *is* Shane's? Are you ready to play step-mommy?"

Joey looked stumped for a moment. She'd been so torn up about what happened that she hadn't even considered it in detail. How would it affect their friendship if he actually had a baby with Kelly?

"That dazed and confused look in your eye tells me you haven't even thought about it,"

Kiko said. "Maybe you shouldn't write Dante off just yet."

"What in the world are you talking about?" Nicole sat forward, genuinely thrown off by Kiko's train of thought.

"Seriously. Let Dante go heal and find someone who wants him," Chelle replied.

"Why you gotta say it like that?" Joey looked to Chelle.

"Because. I doubt he'll ever get your blood-curdling screams out of his head the way you yelled at Shane. I know I won't."

"Men are resilient," Kiko offered.

"And," Chelle continued, glaring at Kiko like she was a rogue agent. "Shane has always come between you and Dante. Even when you first met. Shane will never let you be happy with that man."

"When we first met?"

"You really gonna make me pull your card, huh?" Chelle shook her head as she refilled their wine glasses.

"I'm ready for a good card pulling that ain't about me," Nicole chuckled.

"What are you talkin' about, Chelle?" Kiko took a long sip of her drink.

"Joey? Why don't you tell us what you were up to the night before Kiko's wedding?"

"You mean after the bachelor party?"

"Yes, specifically between the time you were seen leaving the party with Dante and when you showed up to the bridal suite looking tore down."

"I was in my room?"

"With whom?" Chelle led her to answer. "And before you try to lie and say, Dante, I'll tell you I know it wasn't him."

"Ooh, girl. This is better than I thought," Kiko teased.

"How did you know it was Shane?" Joey wasn't even surprised that Chelle had figured out the truth. She just wanted to know how.

"Because you were screaming the man's name at the top of your lungs!"

"Oh," Joey blushed, covering her mouth.

"Y'all use jealousy like foreplay," Nicole said, making them all giggle.

"Like you and Jay ain't dramatic," Joey countered. "Remember, you had your own little secret interlude that weekend."

"Why we bringing up old shit?" Nicole glared at Joey.

"Do tell," Kiko urged. "It seems like everyone was having a ball that weekend, except for me."

June 2009 – After Kiko's Wedding

"Where do you think they're headed off to?" Nicole smirked as the table watched Chelle and Remy stroll out the back door of the banquet room that led to the beach. Joey, Jay, and Shane all grinned, knowing they probably wouldn't be seeing the couple for the rest of the night.

"I bet they're just going to look at the stars," Joey said playfully.

"I bet he's about to make her see stars," Jay joked, and they all laughed.

"It's good to see them together. Warms my heart," Shane added.

The party was winding down, but the DJ was booked for another two hours, and a few people were still getting it in on the dance floor. None of the friends were ready for the night to end, so they sat together, drinking and reminiscing. "Shawty is the Shit" by Dream came on, and Joey jumped up.

"This is my song," she cried out as she began to rock her hips to the beat.

Shane sat there, watching the sexy sway of her body and tried his best not to pounce on her. He knew he couldn't help it, though, and counted to one hundred before jumping up and joining her on the dance floor. Her eyes lit up when she saw him approaching her with the playful look she loved. They always matched each other's energy, whether it was dancing or sneaking off together.

Out of the corner of her eye, she spotted Dante staring at them, but one thing she refused to do was let anyone cramp her style. If he didn't bring his ass on the dance floor to her, then he could watch from the sidelines even though there was something sexy about the intensity of his stare. She held his gaze, and he raised his glass to her and smiled, which earned him a few points with her. Any man that she was with would have to accept her as is.

When she returned her attention to Shane, he glared at her with a glint of determination.

"So, you feeling ole boy?" He nodded toward Dante.

"Maybe. Why?"

"Nothing. Just asking."

"Baby Boy" by Beyoncé came on, and Shane pulled her to him, getting low so he could align with her hips as they swayed together. Joey let go and flowed with the music, body rolling to the melodic groove. Whatever she did, he matched her despite the significant height difference. Then Joey noticed Nicole and Jay heating up the dance floor and began cheering them on, shocked to see her friend let go and have a good time. The fact that Nicole's husband Trey hadn't shown up to the wedding had to be the nail in the coffin of that relationship.

As the reception dwindled, the remaining partygoers agreed to take the party to the hotel bar on the beach. Dante left with the football players, and Joey and Shane hung back with a few other people from college. They all left out the back door of the banquet hall that led to the beach. Shane walked by her side, his hand at the small of her back, drawing small circles along her spine, the slight motion igniting a fire deep inside.

"I'm gonna use the bathroom," she said, waving the group off.
"I'll wait for you," Shane offered, just as she had expected him to.

The bathroom was just inside the long corridor connecting the hotel lobby to the building housing the conference rooms and banquet halls. Joey walked up the ramp leading to the entrance of the building, which had a large archway with a six-foot nook between the door and the ramp. The wall was about three feet back, which created a nice and discreet little hiding spot. Joey led Shane by the hand as she backed up to the wall, then grabbed the middle of his shirt and pulled him to her.

Shane, tired of leaning down, picked her up and pushed her back up against the wall, nuzzling his face in her cleavage before kissing his way up to her lips. Joey bit her lip, trying desperately to contain her moans. Her muffled whimpers were just as seductive to Shane, who had been hard for her since they were on the dancefloor. Visions of the night before had him wanting to bury his dick deep inside her.

"I've been thinking about you all day," he groaned.

Joey wrapped her arms around his neck, gasping when he began to place small bites on her neck and shoulders. She wrapped her legs around his back, rocking her hips into him to try to relieve the aching between her legs the best she could in the bridesmaid's dress. Shane had one hand sliding up her thigh, about to slip a finger past her slit when they heard voices. He placed his other hand over her mouth to stifle her little moans.

"If nothing is wrong, why are you so quiet? You always have something to say." They heard Nicole ask.
"I'm just thinking," Jay answered.

Shane held up one finger for Joey to wait, thinking their friends were just passing by. They remained still, Shane's body pressing her to the wall to keep her up. His finger continued to ease in and out of her, and Joey buried her head in his neck to muzzle her moans.

"I really meant what I said earlier. You may think it's the liquor talking, but it's not," Jay stated.
"Ok," Nicole replied flatly.
"You deserve better, Nick."

"I know that!"

Joey and Shane exchanged a surprised glance when they realized their friends were having more than a friendly conversation. The worst part was that Jay had stopped at the bottom of the ramp where they were hiding. The darkness of the small space concealed them, but if either of their friends came further up the ramp, they'd be busted. So, they remained as still as possible, unwilling witnesses to what sounded like a lover's quarrel.

When it got quiet, Shane leaned back a bit, thinking that they had left, but instead, he saw them kissing. His eyes bulged out of his head, and he gestured for Joey to look. She almost squealed when she peeked over his shoulder and saw what was happening. Knowing her like the back of his hand, Shane kissed her to stifle her outburst.

"I can't," Nicole panted as she tried to catch her breath.

Slowly, Shane let Joey down, motioning for them to be as quiet as possible as they opened the door to the building. Nicole and Jay were kissing again and wouldn't see them.

Once inside, they both took off running, Joey holding back giggles at how goofy Shane looked running in dress shoes, until they reached the lobby. They looked at each other, huffing to catch their breath, and laughed.

"What the fuck?" Shane bellowed, placing his hand on the back of one of the lounge chairs as he controlled his breathing.

"Can you believe that? It was like a Hallmark movie," Joey cackled.

"More like Lifetime with all that damn drama. I feel like we ain't the only ones with a few secrets around here."

"I think that's obvious." Joey plopped down in the chair to take off her shoes.

"You did your thing runnin' in those heels," he laughed.

"Yeah? Well, my feet aren't happy with me right now."

"Wanna go walk on the beach? Cool off in the ocean?" He waggled his brows with mischief.

Before she could answer, Dante came striding through the lobby, stopping when he saw her. Joey couldn't help but stare at him, he was so handsome. He wasn't as tall as Shane, but his six-foot frame filled out his suit just right. He'd taken of his jacket, and his biceps where prominently on display since his shirt fit him like a second skin. Joey didn't quite have a type, but Dante would certainly be on the list.

"Hey, you," he said, glancing between her and Shane. "I was looking for you. I thought you were coming to the bar?"

223

"Oh, I stopped to use the ladies' room. I'm probably gonna turn in early," she replied.

"It has been a long day. I'll walk you to your room. I want to talk to you about something." He extended his arm to help her up, disregarding Shane's presence.

"Um, ok," Joey replied awkwardly, sensing tension between the two men. "I'll see you tomorrow, Shane." Slipping her heels back on, she allowed Dante to escort her to the elevators. She could feel Shane's eyes glaring a hole in her back. As much as she loved him, it was time to start thinking about the future, and Shane had made it clear where they stood.

"Today was crazy. I thought we'd be cuttin' up all day, not playing Love Connection." Joey mused. "What do you think about Chelle and Remy?"

She and Shane were walking on the beach with a couple of drinks from the outside hotel bar. It had been a long day of travel, sprinkled with the drama of Chelle and Remy realizing they'd been broken up over a lie. She sipped her Mojito as the ocean provided the soundtrack for her thoughts.

"Damn," Shane uttered. "Eight years is a long ass time to wonder what happened to your first love. I know that hurt."

"I mean, a lot of shit makes sense now," she replied. "Their weird energy. That night we found her crying."

"That blew my mind to see logical Chelle sobbing like that."

"Right? But I think they're gonna work it out."

"What makes you so sure?"

"Because of graduation night. That wasn't a cute and cuddly kiss. There was some pent-up passion in the way his hand was all tangled up in her hair. They both looked dazed as hell when they broke apart."

Shane laughed. "You know, he would always be watching her but never really said anything. I just thought he had a quiet crush. All this time, he was suffering in silence."

"It was his pride," Joey chuckled. "He shows up at FAMU, per their plan, and she acts like he's got the plague or scurvy. And he doesn't even know why she hates him? That had to be rough."

"I don't know. I think I would have cornered her or something. No way am I gonna see the woman I love and not do anything about it."

Joey was silent after that. As close as they were, they'd both insisted on maintaining their "friends" status even though they'd crossed the line a few times. Their plan had been to focus on their respective goals. The NBA is for him, and a career in communications is for her. Now that they had accomplished that, how would things change between them?

"Why are you so quiet?" Shane nudged her shoulder as they stopped at a pier near the edge of the property.

"I was just thinking. Nothing serious."

"About what?" Shane leveled her with a look that conveyed he knew she was holding back.

"Our friendship and the way everyone speculates about us. We're no better than Chelle and Remy in their eyes."

Shane nodded as he absorbed her words. "Yeah. I mean, it's a little different. We didn't want everyone in our business, judging us. And we had a plan that we agreed not to complicate with the distraction of a relationship."

"True. So now that you're in the NBA, what do you see for yourself?"

"I definitely want a family. I want at least three kids and a house on the beach. Or at least a summer house on the beach."

"And what about your wife?"

"What do you mean? Like, who do I want to be my wife?"

"Not necessarily. How do you see your wife? I know you always said you wanted a stay-at-home mom."

"Yeah. My mother was always gone. Off to some important conference or some mandatory function. I want someone who wants to be dedicated to the kids and the family."

"So, you have to be a stay-at-home mom to be dedicated to your family?"

"I don't see how you could be otherwise."

"I think you can be a mom with a career and still be dedicated to your family, Shane."

"You have a point, but I'm a millionaire. I don't need my wife to work. She can focus on anything she wants, but a corporate career will always take time away from the family. What about you?"

Joey was slightly miffed by his opinion, but she knew his childhood and understood his stance. It was weird because she always swore their feelings for each other went deeper, but his words somehow negated that.

"I eventually want a family. I think a mix of traditional with modern. I love my career, so I'd probably take a sabbatical if and when I got pregnant to stay home with the baby for the first year. I'd want a husband who was able to come home and help with the kids."

"You want a suit," he joked.

"In a perfect world, yes. But he could also be an entrepreneur. Either way, I wouldn't be raising the kids alone."

"Hmm," Shane hummed in response.

The silence stretched between them as they considered each other's words. Shane watched Joey as she stared into her glass like it held the answers to all the questions in the universe. He knew how sensitive she was deep down, and he also knew that he could see her being the mother of his children, but he didn't see a life where she was off dealing with celebrities all day while he was on the road with the kids being raised by nannies. That's how he'd grown up, and refused to put his children through the same thing.

Joey had so many thoughts swirling around in her mind she didn't even know what to feel. Seeing her mother squander her talents because she thought some man was going to take care of her was never too far from her thoughts. Then, having to work to support the kids she had because the men, besides Joey's father, weren't financially able was even worse. Then there was the case of her father. He was so concerned with controlling her with his money that it ruined whatever relationship they could have. Joey knew money was important, but it wasn't everything.

Shane's arm wrapping around her brought her back to reality. She looked up at him as he looked down at her with some unfathomable emotion. Sometimes, he was so easy to read, but other times, like this, she didn't know what was going on in his beautiful head. She wondered what the future had in store for their friendship and hoped that no matter what, they would always have each other.

Chapter 13

A few weeks after her talk with the girls, Joey began to feel like herself again. She returned to the office, and getting back to work helped her take her mind off her personal problems. Dante was gone again, so she didn't have to worry about running into him. The situation was the push she needed to get the ball rolling on starting her own agency or going independent. She didn't need the big machine of the firm behind her; it was just a cushion.

She was sitting at her desk when her cell phone dinged with a call notification from Tori. Joey's brow quirked with curiosity. Tori would call and check up on her from time to time, but typically on the weekends. It was unusual for her to call during the week and certainly not during business hours. Joey wondered if Shane was doing as badly as Chelle relayed, and now his aunt was getting involved.

"Hey, Tori," Joey breathed, trying not to sound too apprehensive.

"Hey, baby. I hate to call you like this, but I have some bad news."

Joey's stomach dropped in an instant. "What's going on?"

"Shane Sr. passed away last night."

"Oh my God. I'm so sorry to hear that," Joey said, feeling the lump form in her throat.

"Thanks, hun. Shane knows, but I can't find him. I've been calling, but he hasn't answered. Can you call him? He'll answer for you. I don't know if his team is aware of what's going on."

"Sure. I'll take care of it."

"Thank you so much. I guess I'll see you soon," Tori replied, her tone thick with grief.

"Again, I'm sorry, Tori. I know you were close with your brother."

"Yeah. He may not have been the best parent, but I know he and Shane were working through things. Please call me when you find him."

"Ok. I will. Love you."

"Love you, too, hun."

After Tori hung up, Joey slouched win her chair. She didn't know that Shane and his father were attempting to reconcile their despondent connection. Over the years, Shane had all but denounced his parents for how uninvolved they had been during his childhood. So, to find out that he'd softened toward his dad meant a lot. She knew he had to be taking the news hard.

She picked up the phone to see if Chelle knew anything.

"Hey, bookie. How are you?"

"I'm ok, but have you talked to Shane?"

"Not in a couple of days. He must be really busy because he hasn't answered my calls since we handled the Kelly situation."

"What happened with Kelly?"

"Oh. You don't know? Girl?"

"What is it?" Joey was frazzled by the news about Shane's father, and anticipation of Chelle's news.

"It's a whole mess. Long story short, Kelly was banging one of the bench players for Phoenix. Her dumb ass thought she could extort Shane for ten million dollars before she had the baby. She didn't expect him to ask for a paternity test. Can you believe it? She asked for the money to keep quiet about your relationship, but she was so eager to get on the payroll that she never read any documents she signed. Not only did she void his contractual obligation to her, but she also forfeited the generous payout she was supposed to receive at the end."

"But how did you know the baby wasn't Shane's?"

"The guy came forward when he found out what she was planning to do. She told him about her contract with Shane, which is how she violated the terms. Bros before hoes, I guess."

Joey slumped back in her seat. Relief, grief, and mental exhaustion knocked her on her ass. She thought about Shane and what he must have been feeling. Her heart ached, and she remembered why she called Chelle in the first place.

"Shane's dad died," Joey sighed. Chelle's gasp triggered the tears she'd been trying to hold back. "Tori just called me. She can't reach him either."

"Shit. Oh my God. Poor Shane." Chelle's voice quivered on the other line.

"We need to contact the team to let them know what's happening."

"Ok. Yeah. He's really making Remy earn his keep. Let me call him and tell him what's going on," Chelle replied.

"Ok. I'll try to figure out where Shane is," Joey replied.

She hung up the phone, knowing instinctively where to find him. Her calendar was still clear for a few more days even though she was in the office, so it wasn't an issue to leave. Grabbing her purse, she pulled out her credit card to book a flight to Laguna Beach. Then, she headed home to pack for a few days.

∞

A car awaited Joey when she landed, and she was reminded of all the trips they had taken to the beach house over the years. Sometimes, it was for his father's parties and other times, it was simply to get away and have alone time with each other. It wasn't even about sex, just the two of them decompressing from the stress of school, internships, and athletic programs. They would hole up for a weekend, binge on their favorite foods, and listen to his father's old records.

Pulling up to the gate, Joey wondered if she should have called first. It had been a few years since she'd been to the house alone, and she wasn't sure if the code was the same. The house was dark and didn't look like anyone was home. Punching in the four digits, she breathed a sigh of relief when the gates clanged open. The driver helped her with her suitcase, and she asked him to hang on in case no one was there.

Allen opened the door before she even rang the bell, and she almost jumped for joy.

"It's good to see you, Joey. Even under such circumstances."

"I know. I wish they were better," she sighed. "Is Shane here?"

"He is, but he's not handling this well. I'm not sure he's eaten any of the food I've served him today."

"Is he in the cigar room?"

"You know he is."

"I'm gonna order some sandwiches. Can you please send them to his bedroom when they arrive?"

"I'll take care of it all. Just go to him. He needs you."

Joey hugged him before toeing off her heels and heading toward the second level. She felt numb, unsure of what to expect or what state Shane would be in when she found him. Her heart began to ache as she recalled how she felt when her grandmother passed and knew that it would be much worse to lose a parent.

The sound of music blasting intensified as she climbed the long staircase. She had gotten stuck in the elevator once and vowed never to take it again. When she reached the top of the stairs, she took a deep breath to ease her apprehension. Slowly, she approached the cigar room, recognizing the song playing. Solomon Burke's crooning of "Cry to Me" served as a reminder of Shane Sr. lauding the praises of oldies ballads and how music has never replicated that depth of emotion in the same way since.

Peeking her head through the door, she found Shane slumped in the leather wingback chair, staring out the window at the endless ocean view. She eased into the room and stood there watching him, his grief evident in his posture and the desolate look in his eyes. They were red-rimmed and bloodshot when he finally noticed her standing there. His shock was rapidly replaced by relief and tears, his head sagging into his hands. Joey rushed toward him and wrapped her arms around him.

Shane clutched at her like he thought she might vanish if he didn't get a good hold of her. He pressed his head into her midsection as the dam burst, and all his emotions flooded out.

Tears trickled from Joey's eyes as he shook in her arms.

"You came," he uttered hoarsely.
She stroked his head. "Of course, I came."

They stayed that way for a while. Him hugging her around the waist, and her rubbing his back and caressing his neck and shoulders. It was almost as if everything that had gone on in the last month didn't exist anymore. None of it mattered. Their bond was too deep and too strong to ever completely turn away from each other.

After a while, he inhaled a ragged breath, turning his head to the side to wipe the wetness from his face. Joey took a step back, finally able to take a good look at him. Her heart ached when she saw just how broken he was. The pain and remorse in his eyes spoke volumes. Getting down on her knees, she cradled his face between her palms. Using her thumbs, she traced the outline of his features, her touch soothed him into closing his eyes and releasing a deep sigh.

"He was just at my last game." Shane's voice was strained and gravelly as he spoke. "We were talking more, you know? He apologized for not being there for me. Said he took for granted that I was destined to be great and focused on giving me the tools. We were gonna plan a fishing trip when the season was over. Now..."

"I'm sorry, baby. I know it hurts." Joey consoled him as she continued to caress his face. "Why didn't you call me?"

"I didn't want to be a burden to you. I knew you would come, even if you didn't want to see me. And I didn't want to do that to you."

"I don't feel like it's a burden. I want to be here for you. With you."

His eyes narrowed as he gazed up at her, wanting to be sure of her meaning. "With me?"

Joey's lips curled up in a small smile as she rubbed her fingers across his eyebrows. "With you."

"Joey."

"I want to be with you. I love you, Shane. I'm always gonna love you. We can figure out the rest."

"You don't have to do this," he uttered. "Please."

The pain in his voice gutted Joey, but she had to let him know how she felt.

"No. I do need to do this now because the moment I saw Tori's name flash on my caller idea, I knew that if you were ok, I wanted to be with you. Nothing else matters. No one else is as important to me as you. Wherever you are is where I wanna be."

"I love you so damn much," he breathed out, grasping the back of her neck as he crashed his lips against hers. His fingers tangled in her hair as his mouth made love to hers. He kissed her like a starving man being served a five-course meal. Like he'd been lost in the desert, and she was the water that would save his life.

When they finally came up for air, they just smiled at each other like two goofy kids. Joey was transported back to the day when he was a tall, lanky boy passing notes to the sassy girl with thick thighs. Overcome, Shane placed quick kisses all over her face until she started giggling.

"Shane!"

"I'm just so happy you're here," he said, placing one last kiss on her nose. "I missed you so bad I couldn't even think straight."

"As upset as I was, I missed you too."

He brushed her long bangs out of her face, tracing the sharp slope of her nose before placing a light tap on the tip. "Tori called you?"

"Yeah. She was worried when she couldn't reach you. Figured I would know how to find you."

"She's always wanted us together."

Joey blew out a breath. "Are you ready for this? For all that's going to come?"

"I can handle it as long as you're with me. Are you ready? What about your clients and –"

"I don't care," she shook her head. "I can do something else. I felt so lost when we didn't speak. And it wasn't even that long."

"Dante?"

"Um... I'm sure you saw him standing outside the restroom at the party. Wasn't really much to say after he heard everything we said. He packed up his shit and left."

Shane huffed. "Good riddance."

Joey just glared at him and shook her head, not even bothering to reason with him that Dante had every right to be upset. Shane just shrugged his shoulders, kissing her hand like she was the most precious thing to him. The automatic record player clicked, and "It's Forever" by The Ebonies was replaced by "I Love You For All Seasons" by The Fuzz, one of Joey's favorite ballads.

"Dance with me?" She rose to her feet and held out her hand to him. Shane nodded as if he was still coming to terms with the fact that things between them had shifted into place. They fit together like a puzzle. Like they always did. Like they were meant to be. For the first time, Joey allowed herself to melt into his embrace totally.

There was no more doubt and no more fear of rejection. Joey allowed her love for Shane to flow from her full force, and she cleaved to his body. Shane encircled her in his long arms, one around her midsection, the other around her shoulder as he crouched down to her height. His fingers played in her hair, and his lips grazed the contour of her ear lobe, holding her close as they danced in the dark.

Eventually, Joey broke away. She walked over to the sound system and pressed the button to have the music playing through the speakers in his bedroom. Taking his hand, she led him through his room and into his bathroom suite. She set the shower to a steaming temperature and lit the lavender-scented candles before turning to him, where he was perched on the sink, watching her with sad eyes. Even though she knew he was happy she was there, Joey could still sense an unsettled vibe coming from him.

"Let's get you undressed," she murmured as she kissed his shoulder.

She pushed off his hoodie and then his T-shirt. Shane stood up so she could finish the task of pulling down his pants and underwear. He stepped out of his clothes and removed his socks. Joey guided him into the shower, letting the rainforest spray shoot from all angles. She quickly removed her clothes and grabbed some fresh washcloths from the cabinet before joining him.

Grabbing his body wash, she began to soap him up from head to toe. She started with gentle swipes across his neck and then worked her way down to his ankles. Emotions were running high, and she felt the lump in her throat increase by the minute. Shane stood still, watching her as she continued to cater to him.

She grabbed the special soap he used for his face and massaged it in before he lifted his face to the warm spray to wash it away. Then she squirted a glob of shampoo in the palm of her hand, lathered up his hair, taking her time to work it through his coils, and followed up with conditioner to tame any tangles.

Eyes closed, Shane let the water run over him to rinse it all away. He made to return the favor, but she pushed his hand away and pushed him back under the spray while she quickly washed herself since she'd showered before her flight. Shane watched her, the hunger in his eyes increasing as she dragged the washcloth over her breasts and then took it from her as she moved to her lady bits. With a gentleness that made her tremble, Shane cleaned each crease and fold.

Joey's breathing picked up as he continued to touch her most intimate places. His eyes held hers as one hand traveled from her waist, up her torso to her breasts. He gripped and plumped her soft globe as his finger teased her nipple to life. She let out a soft cry when he bent forward and sucked the aching peak into his mouth. Slowly, his tongue traced the delicate ridges as his mouth provided just the right friction. His other hand had dropped the washcloth and was caressing her slit while his thumb massaged her clit.

"Shane."

Joey shuddered as her hands reached out to grip his shoulders. The teasing continued as he switched from side to side, sucking and licking the left nipple and then the right. Shane's pace was slow and unhurried. He was driving Joey up a wall as her body began to writhe and chase his touch.

His erection hanging thick and heavy against her stomach had her reeling with need and want. Just when she thought she couldn't take much more, he lifted her against his chest, and she wrapped her legs around him. She gripped the back of his head, kissing him with an intensity that matched her desire.

Shane walked her out of the shower and into the bedroom, laying her on the bed and then sliding in between her thighs that were spread wide open to accommodate him. He kissed in-between her breasts before wrapping one hand around one and nibbling and licking the other. Joey shoved her fingers in his damp hair as she arched her back so that she could press her mound against him, aching to feel him inside of her. He pushed her legs over his shoulders as he placed his lips just below her belly button and kissed his way down. Her body quivered in anticipation and convulsed when the heat of his tongue against her clit sent waves of pleasure through her.

Her body writhed with need as she guided his head right where she needed it, desperate to be filled, whether it was his finger, tongue, or his dick. Sucking her clit until her back bowed off the bed and she begged for more, he stuck his tongue as deep inside her as it could go. His satisfied moans grew louder as his arousal stiffened, and her essence dripped down his chin as she came apart.

Kissing his way up her body, Shane lifted her leg around his waist as he entered her still-spasming pussy. He moaned her name as she let out a ragged cry as he began to roll his hips.

"I need you," he whispered against her lips.

"Mhm, need you too," she moaned.

"Don't leave me,"

She wrapped her arms around his neck, squeezing him tight. "I'll never leave," she promised.

"I love you, Jonelle. I always have."

Tears sprang up in Joey's eyes as Shane continued pouring his heart out to her. The frenzy died down, and their bodies enjoyed a languid dance. He cradled her in his arms as he took his time drawing out her orgasm, peppering her with tender kisses and heartfelt words of love and devotion. Their tears mingled as their love bound them even tighter than before.

Junior Year (2006)

In honor of the basketball team advancing to the NCAA playoffs, a big party was held in one of the school's frat houses. Joey and the crew were there to celebrate, all standing around in the kitchen, drinking and talking. The topic of conversation flowed to which celebrity was their type. Remy had just said Nia Long was his crush, then Shane squinted and remarked that Chelle highly resembled the actress.

There had been some back and forth after Remy denied seeing the similarity, and then Chelle floored the room by saying Remy wasn't her type because she liked a more manly type like her boyfriend, Tony. Shane had said Ashanti was his type, but his eyes kept landing on Joey, who said Denzel Washington was hers.

After a while, the group separated to do their own thing. Joey was enjoying herself, dancing with as many people as she could. Over the years, she'd garnered a reputation for being a big flirt. While she dated a lot, she wasn't necessarily known to sleep around. But you knew that if she was there, it would be a good time. She and Shane were the life of the party, always laughing and joking. He had grown into his looks and gained some muscle mass and more and more female attention. But, like Joey, he wasn't interested in any relationship that would distract him.

Ever since she moved out of his room, they'd been good about following the rules they set for their friendship. She even spent the night in his room occasionally if they had a late study night or she was tipsy and forgot she didn't live there anymore. Well, at least until the night she showed up, and he had a half-naked girl in his bed. After that, Joey was careful that they didn't cross the boundaries. People always questioned their closeness, but since they dated other people, their "just friends" status was accepted.

"You Got It Bad" by Usher was playing, and couples were grinding on each other on the makeshift dance floor in the living room of the frat house. Joey was swaying by herself, with a captive audience of guys who were either too shy or still working up the courage to ask her to dance. She was in her zone, enjoying the sexy ballad, when someone came up behind her. She knew who it was because no one smelled like him. Shane's signature scent, Dior Homme, blended well with his body chemistry. Joey loved getting hugs from him because his scent always lingered.

He was so much taller that he always had to stoop lower to dance with her from behind. Joey could feel the familiar heat radiating between them as they rocked back and forth to the music. The way his strong hands gripped her by the waist and then slid up and down her body had her biting her lip; she was so turned on.

She placed her hands over his, guiding them where she wanted to be touched. There was just something about Shane that always dismantled her defenses.

Joey turned to face him, wrapping her arms around his neck and pulling his head closer so she could whisper, "Let's go back to your room."

"Yours is closer," he replied. "I'll give you a head start."

Joey smiled and slipped out the backdoor of the party, knowing there would be fewer people to deal with. She didn't see anyone in their immediate circle, so no one would suspect that she and Shane were up to anything. When she reached her dorm building, she waited by the entrance to let him in. It was late, and no one was outside when he strolled up to the door. They took the staircase up to the second floor, stopping to make out and grope each other along the way.

When they tumbled out of the stairwell, Joey grabbed his hand and led him to her door. He stood behind her, his hands up her skirt, as she fished her key out of her small crossbody purse. When she pushed the door open, she was shocked to see Chelle spread across her bed, crying. Joey could have sworn she was with Tony.

"Girl! What happened?" Joey seemed confused and concerned as she approached Chelle's bed. Shane just stood by the door.

"Nothing. You guys didn't have to come looking for me," Chelle said as she swiped at her eyes.

Joey glanced over to Shane, who shrugged his shoulders, perplexed.

"Why are you crying? We were laughing and having a good time one minute, and the next, you were gone."

"I think I know," Shane spoke up. He closed the door and sat at the foot of Chelle's bed. "It's about Remy. Right?"

"Remy?" Joey sounded puzzled. "What does he have to do with it?"

"Keep up, Joey. They dated in high school," he replied.

"Ok, and?" Joey shrugged. "That was forever ago, and they barely talk to each other now."

"Exactly. I've always thought it was bullshit, and the way they are so awkward around each other tells me that we're missing something. It hurt your feelings when he said you weren't his type." Shane rubbed Chelle's shoulder, and she nodded. She couldn't believe he had read between the lines when even her friend had missed it.

"Hurt whose feelings? Chelle's?" Joey was still lost because Chelle acted like she didn't care about anything. "Chelle wassup baby? I'ma need you to use your words cause I thought you said he wasn't that special."

They sat there and listened as Chelle recounted her true feelings for Remy and what really went down between them. She made them promise never to tell anyone, to which they both offered a pinky. After getting things off her chest, Chelle decided to call Tony. Joey and Shane said they were heading back to the party, which was code for the fact that they were heading to his room.

As they walked across the campus, less concerned that anyone would see them at that late hour, Joey felt wetness splattering across her forehead and the back of her legs. She looked up at Shane, who was swiping water off his eyebrow. They exchanged a wary glance, and both picked up the pace. Just like Florida's unpredictable weather, it went from mist to an all-out downpour in minutes.

Shane grabbed Joey's hand as they jogged across the quad through the rain, pulling her under a giant oak tree-covered bench. Accepting the fact that they were soaked, Joey pushed Shane into the seat and straddled him. They resumed their passionate kissing and touching like they hadn't just spent the last hour consoling their friend.

Shane's hands were inside of her skirt, groping her luscious thighs, and Joey's hands were at the waistband of his sweats. When he grabbed her hand and directed it to his rock-hard erection, they both gasped when she squeezed it.

Somewhere along the way, they'd made a silent agreement to take things all the way. At least it seemed that way because he didn't stop her from stroking him, she didn't stop him from pulling her panties to the side and twisting her clit, and he didn't stop her from raising up and guiding his shaft inside of her. They absorbed each other's moans as their lips locked and tongues tangled.

Joey fucked Shane fast and furious on that bench in the rain. She bounced up and down in such a succinct rhythm he could only grip her waist and hold on. Her soft ass cheeks slamming against his thighs made him grunt with each downward motion. When he felt her begin to clamp around his dick, he thrust upward to meet her, and she cried out as her orgasm bloomed in her core. Joey threw her head back and moaned like a wild woman, causing Shane to erupt right along with her.

They stayed that way for a short while, letting the rain shower down on them as they kissed and came back down to earth. Neither one articulated it, but they both felt a shift in their feelings, knowing that they had surpassed friendship or even messing around. It was one of those moments in time when they both knew that things would never be the same again.

Chapter 14

Present

The next few weeks were equally challenging and transformative for Joey. She had to speak with Stew to tell him the truth about her and Shane. She filled him in on some of their backstory and also informed him of the situation with Kelly regarding the paternity of her child. More like fake paternity. They couldn't keep the fact that Kelly was pregnant from the media, and there would be wild speculation. With their contract being up, Shane didn't have to pretend to be with Kelly any longer, and while the contract itself wasn't the best idea, the ten-year NDA that Chelle had insisted Kelly sign ensured that she wasn't able to discuss the terms of their fake relationship and subsequent breakup.

They were still careful about appearing places together, though. Joey was by his side for his father's funeral, but so were all his college friends. It was common knowledge that Joey was his publicist and that they had history going back to their FAMU days, so it wasn't far-fetched that she would be there. Joey did her best to keep things under wraps to minimize media coverage. Per Shane Sr.'s request, his ashes were sprinkled in the ocean behind the Laguna Beach house.

After the ceremony, the friends who didn't have to fly back home spent the remainder of the weekend at the house. Joey had Allen arrange catering and massage appointments for the crew. Joey, Shane, Chelle and Remy lounged around, talking and reminiscing while Jay and Nicole went for a walk on the beach. Everyone was thrilled that Joey and Shane finally made things official. The foursome hung out in the cigar room, the guys smoking while Chelle rummaged through the extensive record collection. Once she found it, she ranted on and on about feeling slighted. She was just finding out about it.

"I honestly can't understand how you two scoundrels never showed me this room!" Chelle examined an album cover, recognizing it as a Motown collector's edition of Marvin Gaye's "Grapevine" and slipped out the record to add it to the automatic player. "Stay in My Corner" by The Dells played as Joey sang her heart out. Chelle joined her, linking hands as they emulated an old-school slow dance. The guys watched from the balcony, amused by their antics.

"I don't know if I've ever seen Joey this happy," Remy noticed. "Even despite the craziness of the last few months."

Shane smiled and nodded. Even though his father's funeral had been a few days prior, he felt a deep sense of peace washing over him. "She's the happiest person I've ever known. With the things she's been through? Most people would have become jaded or cold. Joey just stuck to her vision and did what most people can't do."

Remy blew a puffed ring of smoke over the balcony. "What's that?"

"She was committed to doing things her way. Everything that's coming together now, down to us all being in the same locale, was part of her vision. Falling in love and the traditional relationship draw didn't work for her."

"But she did fall in love. Right?" Remy looked him in the eye. "This didn't just happen. You two have been carrying these feelings for a long time."

"That's my point. She put jealousy and fear of losing me to the side. She was willing to accept being my friend if that meant we both could realize our dream of becoming who we wanted to be."

"And you don't think you could have done that as a couple?"

"I doubt it. We both needed that space to explore, I think. When I first moved to Arizona, it really hit me who she was to me. And I didn't handle it well. The whole time, I'm fuckin' up, and Joey's calmly laying out a strategy for me to get back on track. As my friend who knew me and understood me. I know it sounds crazy, but it's hard to explain."

"So, what's next?" Remy raised an expectant brow.

Shane just smiled and shrugged. "I make her the happiest woman in the world or die trying."

Inside, the girls were chatting between singing and dance breaks. Chelle had a million questions about situations she needed Joey to fill in the blanks for. She remembered suspicious situations involving Joey and Shane and wanted to verify if her instincts were right despite how many times Joey had said they were "just friends."

"So that night you found me crying over Remy. Were you really looking for me?"

Joey blushed, remembering how the night ended. "Sorry, friend. I thought you were with Tony and planned on using the room for a quickie."

"You heifer!" Chelle laughed. "How about the weekend of Nicole's birthday? Were y'all creepin' in the bushes?"

Joey smirked. "We heard Kelly in the kitchen and thought Jay's room was the one Nicole wasn't using."

"But I thought you were pissed at him about that whole situation?"

"I was, but I don't know. I guess seeing each other with someone else just made us crazy."

"Yeah. Jealousy as foreplay." Chelle shook her head. "Just friends, my ass. Whole time y'all having a whirlwind relationship!"

"That's a little dramatic," Joey chuckled.

"It's the damn truth!" Chelle wagged a finger at Joey. "Shane would act like it didn't bother him to see you dancing or hanging out with other guys, but every time he winds up dancing with you, you guys would magically disappear. Did you honestly think you were fooling me? Maybe some of the group. Nicole was busy dealing with Trey, and Kiko was consumed with Dom, but I'm your bestie."

"I'm sure Jay knew too. He tried to talk to me first, but Shane told him I was off-limits. He also caught us making out a few times."

"How?"

"Well," Joey braced herself for Chelle's reaction. "I was living in Shane's dorm room most of our first semester."

"What?" Chelle's outburst caught the guys' attention, and they both looked up in confusion. She waved them off and then rounded on Joey. "Are you kidding me? As his girlfriend? Or what?"

Joey told her the whole story about her grandmother and the funeral, how Shane and his aunt stepped in like they were family, how that was what really brought her and Shane together, and why he was so territorial over her.

"It's not like I didn't know he had feelings for me. I just knew he wouldn't do anything to jeopardize our friendship. And," Joey looked over her shoulder to make sure the guys weren't listening or paying attention to them. "I overheard a conversation between him and Tori. She basically told him to play the part of my friend until the time was right."

"Wow," Chelle exclaimed in awe. "You guys are truly soulmates."

"Marriage has seriously made you all soft and googly-eyed," Joey teased.

"But, you didn't deny it," Chelle laughed.

"True."

"And now is the time?"

Joey looked out the patio door at Shane lounging in his chair, looking more relaxed than he'd been in a while. He glanced up and caught her watching him. He blew her a kiss, which she caught and placed her hand over her heart.

"Oh my God, I think I'm gonna cry," Chelle huffed with a hand over her chest, overwhelmed with her friends' display of sweetness.

"Stop," Joey giggled. Then she noticed wetness at the corner of Chelle's eyes. "Wait! Are you really crying? Chelle?"

"I'm so damn happy for you, that's all," she replied, dabbing the corners of her eyes. "And it's so obvious how in love you two are. I just wish I got to see more of it."

"You will! Now you get to see the best of it." Joey's voice cracked as she considered what her future held in store.

"And you deserve it. I couldn't love you more if you were my real sister," Chelle sniffed as she wrapped her arms around Joey. The two girls hugged each other tight. Both were overjoyed that they found love despite enduring rocky beginnings. Chelle had secretly yearned for Remy for over ten years, and Joey had harbored a secret love for Shane for almost as long.

"What are you two doing?" Remy asked as he walked up and embraced both women, hugging Chelle from behind and placing an arm around Joey's shoulder.

"I don't think we want to know," Shane chuckled, noticing Chelle's red-rimmed eyes. He extended his long arms around the trio and yelled, "Group hug!"

Freshman year - January 2004

Shane tossed a basketball in the air and then from hand to hand as he watched Joey pack up her things. He bopped his head to "Why I Love You" by B2K while she danced around the room, ensuring she got all her stuff. It was the start of the new semester, and she could finally move on campus. Joey had grown close to Nicole and her best friend, Chelle, and decided to move in with them because she didn't want to room with strangers.

"I'm gonna miss you, Juicy."

"Stop callin' me that!" Joey chuckled. It was a name he'd started calling her because of her thighs and the waterpark he said resided between them.

"I'm not going away. Just getting out of your hair. I'm sure you'll be happy to have your privacy back to jerk off or whatever," she teased.

"I do that regardless." He shrugged when she glared at him and then laughed when she attempted to punch his arm. "Stop! I'm just kidding!"

"You're so nasty!"

"You ain't seen nothin'." He waggled his eyes suggestively.

"What is wrong with you today? You need to get laid?" Joey returned to gathering her toiletries and putting them in the designated tote. With Jay's help, they planned to pack everything in Shane's car and drive it over to the girl's dorm.

"I need a girlfriend," he sang in the vein of Bobby Brown.

"I know a couple of girls I know would kill for the chance," she suggested.

Shane cut his eyes at her. "I don't need your help finding a girl."

"I was just offering my services."

"What else are you offering?" His breath tickled her neck as he leaned behind her to ask the question, startling her because she didn't realize he was so close.

"What are you talking about?" She asked, even though she knew exactly what he was referring to because her body had reacted to his words. In an instant, her panties were soaking wet, and her nipples pebbled against her FAMU hoodie.

Shane wrapped an arm around her, which happened to rub across her already sensitive peaks, and pulled her against him so she could feel his erection. "You know what I'm talking about."

"Shane," she said, like a warning. "I'm not going there with you again."

"You don't have to do anything except bend over and let me drown for a lil bit."

"Don't use me cause you're horny!" She cackled as he attempted to pull her sweats down.

"You're the reason I'm horny. Be for real!"

He playfully pushed her on the bed when she wouldn't let him in her pants. Joey rolled on her back, still laughing at him until he dove on top of her. They wrestled as he pretended he was going to undress her against her will. Joey shrieked when he started to tickle her to get her to move her hands.

"Shane!"

"Shane!" Jay's voice scared them both as he mimicked Joey. Shane sagged on the bed in defeat, and Joey shoved him away from her as she jumped to her feet.

"Oh, good. You're here."

"Yes, I am. You guys told me to help you pack. Should I come back?"

"Nope. I'm basically ready. You guys can start packing up the car.

Shane's groan drifted up from the bed, where he was still lying face down. "Give me a minute."

Jay chuckled, seeming to understand what his boy meant, grabbed her suitcases and walked out. Joey did one last sweep of the room, checking that she didn't leave anything behind. She laughed at Shane, who had finally rolled over and was adjusting his retreating erection.

"You couldn't at least leave me with a parting gift?"

"You damn right, it's a gift," she chuckled. "And you don't get to decide when I give it."

"I don't like that rule," he grumbled.

"Well, get used to it. Friend!"

Joey felt a sense of belonging when they arrived at the girls' dorm. Nicole and her best friend, Chelle, embraced her and were just as excited for her to join them, making her feel good. Moving back and forth as a child, she was usually the odd man out, so making friends who felt like sisters was a dream come true.

Chelle was in the room when Joey arrived, and together, they directed the boys on where to put everything. In the middle of the mayhem between placing Joey's things and moving Chelle's around, Nicole walked in. Jay immediately took notice of her and began to lose focus.

"Hey, Nicole." All the girls froze at his deep baritone voice. They knew him from being on the basketball team and that he was popular with the girls on campus, but they had never heard him use that tone.

"Don't say my name like that," Nicole scoffed.

"Why?" Jay folded his arms across his chest as he smirked down at her.

"Because. I don't like it."

"I don't believe that. I think you don't want to like it."

She held up her finger and wagged it, showing off her finger. "I'm married. I don't need to like it."

Their friends laughed as Shane ribbed Jay for his first defeat. Chelle and Joey giggled as Jay tried to pretend that his ego didn't take a hit, but before they left, he was able to cajole her into giving him a hug. Then the girls got on her for giving in to his charms. Joey offered to order pizza as a reward for their help, which they agreed to eat in Shane's room since he had a lounge area and more room. She couldn't help but feel joy as they all piled into his car. Their eyes met in the rearview mirror, and he returned her smile. She could feel the start of something special brewing, and she liked it.

Chapter 15

Present

At first, things were quiet. They kept a low profile, doing the things famous people do when they don't want to draw attention to themselves, like arriving at places separately, never driving in the same car together, and staying away from anywhere popular or where paparazzi hung out. That worked for them, but it became more difficult once word spread that Shane was no longer dating Kelly. He was a hot commodity in the league, a sexy single player with a new contract. Of course, everyone wanted to know who he would be with next.

The first time they were spotted, they were returning from Shane's game in San Francisco on a private Jet. Someone must have tipped off the media because when they exited the airport, they were met with incessant camera flashes in their face. Within hours, the rumor of their "budding" relationship was all over the internet.

They had already discussed the backlash of becoming a couple in the public eye, and Joey had already resigned from her position at the agency. Much like she embraced her love for

Shane, she also decided to pursue her love of dancing and added a few choreography classes to her schedule. She realized that the corporate world she had always coveted could be a cold, cruel place, and she didn't want to waste any more time restricting herself from what made her happy. Stew offered her an opportunity as a consultant to provide her unique strategies as a service to their high-profile clients. Joey was good with that as long as she wasn't required to show up to the office.

By the time the college reunion rolled around, their status as a couple was well-known. Of course, there were rumors about how long they had been dating and whether Joey was the reason for Shane's breakup. Since Kelly wasn't talking, the buzz eventually died down. Of course, people who knew them in college came out of the woodwork with stories about how everyone knew they were together. Someone had even written a blog post about how Joey and Kelly had fought over Shane back in the day. Random pictures of them together over the years were flooding all the hottest blogs and gossip sites.

They showed up late for the actual reunion celebration because of an exhibition game Shane had played in Greece a few days prior. There was no way Joey was passing up the chance to travel to one of the countries on her bucket list, and they had spent the previous day sightseeing. Walking into the venue hand in hand, the crowd started to buzz since Shane was easily recognizable. People who knew them personally began to clap and cheer since the big question the four years they attended FAMU had always been, "Are you guys a couple?"

They passed Nicole and Jay on the dance floor, slow grinding to "You" by Lloyd. Joey laughed at how they were so lost in each other that they didn't notice their friends watching them. When Nicole finally looked up, she squealed and grabbed Joey, pulling her in for a hug while still backing it up on her fiancé. Jay exchanged a knowing grin with Shane as they did their special handshake from their days of playing ball together.

The couple made their way around the ballroom, finding Chelle and Kiko talking at a table in the back while Remy and Dom were at the bar. Both women jumped up and rushed Joey like they hadn't seen each other in years, not just a couple of months earlier at the funeral. Everyone was ecstatic that Joey and Shane were out in the open. They'd all been secretly rooting for the *secret* couple.

There was no shortage of people wanting to talk to Shane, Dom and Jay, or even ask for pictures and autographs. After the initial frenzy subsided, the crew did what they did best and enjoyed the party. Joey and Shane, naturally the life of the party, seemed even more on fire since they could be free with each other. They danced together as usual, but now they could flirt and kiss, singing the lyrics of certain songs to each other at the top of their lungs. It was almost as if they wanted the whole world to know how in love they were.

Like when "I Know What You Want" by Busta Rhymes and Mariah Carey played. Shane acted out all the male lyrics to Joey while she sang and rapped from the female's point of view. He touched and caressed her body sensually while she acted seductive yet coy. Then "Lovers and Friends" by Lil John came on, and he really acted out.

Of course, the girls took full advantage of being together, dancing, and cutting up with each other. It was just like old times as they performed for the crowd. Everyone eager to be transported back to their best years, even if just for one night. When "Soldier" by Destiny's Child played, Chelle hyped them up as they did one of their favorite cheer routines.

Soon, the people on the dance floor crowded around as they put on a show. Nicole mouthed the lyrics since Jay was the most hood dude in the crew. She saluted Jackson, who was sipping a drink and enjoying the performance. Chelle sang about the soldiers from the BK, and Kiko pointed at Jackson when the part about a reformed D Boy played and then went to dance on Dom. The ladies in the crowd went wild because Jackson was a fan favorite. Joey sang about the type that might change her life, and

Shane nodded as he wrapped an arm around her shoulder.

"One Wish" by Ray J slowed the party back down, and Shane sought Joey out and made a dramatic show of asking her to dance. Joey accepted his hand like she always did, and he twirled her around a few times before pulling her close. They rocked back and forth as he whispered the lyrics in her ear. Joey smiled to herself, remembering how he used to sing the song all the time, and she would imagine that that's how he felt about her.

"You love me?" Shane asked against her earlobe.

"You know I do," she whispered back.

"This is forever," he said before stepping back.

Joey's expression was of confusion when he just stopped dancing in the middle of the dance floor. She looked around to see if someone had interrupted them or bumped him, but her eyes bugged out of her head when he lowered to one knee. Shane smiled up at her as he flipped open a small black velvet box, revealing a ring with a rock in the middle that was so big it almost blinded her as it reflected the lights around them like a disco ball.

"Shane!" Joey squealed in shock. "Shane!"

"Joey," he said once she stopped screaming. "Jonelle, my love. I've been in love with you since the day you checked that box in our first-period English class. Even though I wasn't sure how I would do it, my mission was to convince you to love me back. Now that I know, without a doubt, that I can't live without you, I need you to join me as my best friend forever and be my wife. Will you marry me?"

The wild smile on her face and the pounding of her heart couldn't keep the tears at bay. Joey, too overcome to speak, nodded frantically as she extended her hand for him to slip on the five-carat, heart-shaped, canary yellow Harry Winston diamond ring with half-moon baguettes on each side. Joey's eyebrows went sky-high when she examined the ring up close. The quality was flawless, and she had heart palpitations when calculating how much the ring must have cost. It hit her for the first time that she was marrying her best friend, who just signed a sixty-million-dollar contract. She looked in total shock at her girls, who were now surrounding her.

"Chelle," she gasped as she shoved the ring in her friend's face. "Is this real?"

Chelle laughed as she attempted to get her friend to calm down. "Yes, bookie. It's real."

"Girl!" Nicole screamed when she got a good look at the ring. "That's a good man, Savannah!" She quoted from Waiting to Exhale.

"I love everything about this," Kiko sighed as she wrangled Joey out of Nicole's embrace and threw her arms around her. "I still remember the first time you guys saw each other that day in cheer practice. I've known since then!" She kissed Joey on both cheeks and grabbed Shane's hand to bring him into the hug.

"That's what I'm talkin' about," Remy said as he clapped his hands then clapped his boy on the chest in congratulations.

"Finally!" Jay's deep voice boomed, and then, "Got damn!" when he saw the ring.

The DJ congratulated the couple as he played "Adore" by Prince, per Chelle's request. Everyone watched the couple come together, but this time was different than all the other times they had danced together before. Joey looked up at Shane like he was her actual knight in shining armor. A dream come true. She couldn't believe how lucky they were to have found each other at such a young age and weather the ups and downs of coming of age together. Tears stung her eyes as their special moments, secret or not, flashed in her mind.

"I love you so much," she mouthed.

The storm of emotions swirled in Shane's eyes as he nodded and replied, "I'll love you forever."

∞

After the reunion, the group boarded a private jet to the Bahamas to spend a week together for Shane's upcoming birthday. He suggested they upgrade their trip from the

Airbnb on Miami Beach to a Caribbean island instead. They couldn't just do things and go to certain places without it being fodder for entertainment or gossip, and Miami would have been a shit show with him, Dom, and Jay being in the same place.

Instead, they rented a large palatial house on a private beach with eight bedrooms, a movie theater, indoor and outdoor pools, a tennis court, and indoor and outdoor basketball courts. Even though most of them were used to that kind of luxury, or something close, the crew still ran through the house like little kids, excited with each new luxury amenity they discovered. They chose their rooms and turned in early since it had been a long day for most of them.

Shane and Joey were jet-lagged, having endured international travel just to get to the party. They both had just enough energy to shower and crawl into bed. Despite being tired and up for almost twenty-four hours, they found sleep elusive.

He spooned her from behind, skimming one hand up and down her thighs while the other entwined with hers as she held his arm to her chest. Joey was comforted by his soft touch and his breathing against her ear. She could feel his heart beating at a calm rate with his chest pressed up against her back.

"I'm so tired, I can't even get hard," he sighed while holding her tighter and pressing a kiss to the back of her head.

Joey chuckled. "That's a first. But if you did get hard, you'd be doing all the work because my body is tied!"

"It was worth it, though. I wasn't sure what to expect, but I think the night was epic."

"Did you plan on proposing at the party? Cause it seemed like nobody knew."

"I played around with the idea. I almost did it in Greece, but figured I'd wait until the party. Then, this feeling came over me, and it felt like the right time. I was dancing with you, and you had this satisfied smile on your face, and for the first time, it clicked that I made you as happy as you made me. I sometimes feel like I love you more."

Joey turned to face him, sliding her arms around his neck. "You couldn't possibly think that."

"I really thought I lost you. When I saw how you reacted to Kelly being pregnant, you wouldn't talk to me. You always talk to me, Joey. Even if you're mad as hell. Even if it's to tell me I'm a fuckin' idiot. But you refused to even look at me."

Joey stroked the back of his neck while he talked. When he stated his fear of losing her, her eyes closed at the thought of how much pain she felt.

"For the first time, I allowed myself to embrace my feelings for you and be excited about our future together, and then she showed her belly, and it felt like I was splintering on the inside. My heart and mind split, and I literally felt like I was gonna lose my mind. I had to leave the room because I had visions of attacking you."

"Me? Not her?"

"No. I don't care about Kelly, but I'd catch a charge over you. You're the one that got her pregnant even as you promised me we would be together forever."

"I didn't get her pregnant," he said firmly.

"We know that now, but at the time, I didn't know what was going on."

"I'm just glad that shit's over and we can put it behind us. I don't know what she was thinking, attempting to extort me for what I would have given her if she'd just asked."

"That's what you get for picking her slow ass in the first place," Joey said dryly.

"Aww! Are you Jealous, Chunk?" He kissed her on the nose, laughing when she turned her head.

"Don't you dare start calling me that again!"

"You used to love that name," he chuckled.

"Yeah, until I started to resemble it," she laughed.

"Please. You are thick as hell, and I love that shit. Give me all of this shit right here," he said as he gripped and jiggled her stomach, ass and thighs.

"I love it too. Just don't call me that."

"Ok, Shawty."

"And how do you call me that and Chelle that too?"

"No, Chelle is Shorty because she's short. You my Shawty."

"Hmm. Ok," Joey mumbled, rolling her eyes.

Shane grabbed his phone and connected it to the Bluetooth speakers in their room. He opened his music player app and scrolled until he found Plies. "Shawty" began to play, and he stood in bed as he rapped the lyrics.

"Even though I'm not your man, you're not my girl, I'ma call you my Shawty!"

Joey giggled, trying to get him to hush as he continued to sing and act out the entire song. He pulled her up until they were both dancing and laughing together. He slid an arm around her while he rapped about his Shawty and everything they did. The song was reminiscent of the beginning of their friendship when he had her back and would do anything for her. It was also reminiscent of how they both grew together mentally and sexually, teaching each other how they liked to be pleased.

Then "Shawty is Da Shit" by Dream came on, and Joey squealed because she loved that song.

"Take y'all asses to bed!" Jay's muffled voice boomed from the other side of their door. Joey froze, frightened by the sudden outburst, but then dissolved into laughter as Shane began to sing even louder.

Together, they danced and bounced on the bed, singing songs that reminded them of each other until true tiredness kicked in, and they collapsed back onto the mattress, cuddling each other until the sound of their heavy breathing was all that could be heard.

∞

On their first morning in the Bahamas, Joey and Shane were the last to wake up, finding the rest of their friends up and active by 10:00 a.m. Chelle was cleaning the kitchen so their catered breakfast could be set up. Nicole and Kiko made mimosas, and Jay, Dom, and Remy tossed a football around on the beach. Shane waved to the ladies as he headed outside to join the guys.

"Good morning, friends," Joey bellowed as they joined the girls.

"Well, someone's bright and chipper this morning," Nicole mused.

"I wonder why that could be," Chelle feigned confusion.

"Do your mornings start with a club performance? Because I know the night ended with one," Kiko joked.

"You heard us? What kind of thin-ass walls does this place have?"

"Huh?" Chelle was confused for real.

"Last night. They had a whole concert going on," Kiko replied.

"Jay said he heard them when he went to the kitchen to get us some drinks," Nicole chuckled.

"I'm just trying to figure out whether you were in the closet or outside our bedroom door, too," Joey said to Kiko, scratching her head.

"Dom and I were outside and heard the music. Your room is facing the beach," Kiko clarified.

"And what were y'all doing on the beach after dark all alone? Hmm?" Nicole couldn't help but ask.

Kiko rolled her eyes. "Nothing as exciting as this ring! Let me see it close up," she said as she reached for Joey's hand to admire her engagement ring. Chelle and Nicole exchanged a glance, noticing how Kiko had changed the subject.

"This all feels like a dream," Joey sighed as she looked at the stunning rock on her hand. She glanced outside to see Shane catch the football, laughing at something Jay said before tossing it back to Dom. The smile on his face warmed her heart, even as his tall, muscular body covered in tats warmed other areas.

"Aww," Nicole cooed. "Being in love looks good on you."

"Right," Chelle agreed. "I hate that we didn't get to see it at full capacity all these years. When this all dies down, I'm gonna beat both your asses for wasting my time!"

"I know the pot ain't calling the kettle black," Kiko laughed. "Nobody beat yours or Remy's ass, so we'll give Joey and Shane a pass."

They all looked at Nicole, who shrugged and threw her hands up.

"Hey, I'm keeping my mouth shut. I have nothing to say but congratulations booski."

"It's bookie!" Both Chelle and Joey cried out.

"You know what I meant!" Nicole laughed as she passed around glasses of champagne and orange juice. "Oh, wait. Nobody's pregnant, right?"

They looked at each other suspiciously as they each took a tentative sip, giggling when they confirmed that no one was. The caterers finished arranging their brunch spread, which consisted of traditional breakfast items like pancakes, waffles, French toast, bacon, sausages, scrambled eggs, and fruit. They also had grits, biscuits, sausage gravy, hash browns, steak, and a station to make breakfast tacos.

As usual, Joey was the first to grab a plate and pile it with a little of everything she liked. Chelle called the guys in, and they all sat around the large dining table, eating and catching up. Nicole facetimed her mother, who was staying at her house in Miami watching the babies. She seemed to be having a ball with the boys, who were crawling all over her so that they could talk to their mommies on the little phone screen.

"So, y'all took fifty-leven years to become official. How long are we gonna have to wait for a wedding?" Dom asked as he sat with his arm draped over the back of Kiko's chair as his fingers threaded through her long ponytail.

"Uh," Joey hummed. "I guess we have to plan that out. We are only twelve hours into the engagement."

"*Shid*," Shane breathed out as he leaned back in his chair. He looked Joey in her eyes as he said, "We'd get married tomorrow if it were up to me."

Kiko's eyes ballooned, and her brows hit her hairline as she took his words literally. "You could actually do that! Why don't you guys get married here?"

"Because that's crazy," Joey said.

"No, think about it. A beautiful wedding on the beach. All your friends are already here. Well, all the important ones. And if you want, you can throw a party to celebrate once you return to Cali."

The room fell silent as they waited for Joey's rebuttal. She looked to Shane, hoping he would back her up, but he gave her that goofy smile that meant he was considering something crazy.

"You like this idea?"

He shrugged. "I mean, I would have to fly Tori down, but everyone I care about is already here. I like the idea of planning an official reception when we get back. We're rarely all in the same place at the same time."

"And it's your birthday," Chelle added.

"That's right," Jay's voice boomed from the opposite end of the table. "Your birthday is in two days."

"If anyone can put together a wedding in two days, it's Kiko," Remy cosigned.

"Thank you, Remy. Especially with Nicole and Chelle's help." Kiko nodded proudly.

"This is so exciting," Nicole chimed in, clapping her hands.

"And we can fly in anything you need, but I'm sure we can find everything on the island," Dom added.

"I love this so much," Chelle sighed.

"Are you guys serious?" Joey looked around the room in awe as she processed the enormity of what was happening.

Shane leaned forward in his chair and took her hands in his. "I'm ready if you are. As a matter of fact, I've been ready."

"Well," she sighed. "I guess we're doing this!"

The room erupted in claps and cheers as Shane gathered Joey in his arms and kissed her with such passion their friends looked away after a while. One of the guys clearing their throat snapped Shane back to reality. He was so happy; he felt like he could kiss her forever. Joey swiped at the tears slipping down her cheeks as she accepted a barrage of hugs from her girlfriends.

Kiko wasted no time jumping into action. After brunch, the girls went downtown to see if they could find a dress on the island or if they would have to order one. Joey wasn't sure she would be able to find anything off the rack to flatter her fuller curves, but they were directed to a special dressmaker who worked with a boutique that specialized in unique wedding dresses. She tried on two dresses before she found the one that was almost perfect for her. It had a halter neck with a deep V in the cleavage. The dress was short with a long detachable train that ruffled from the waist to her hips.

"I think I'm in love," she said in a daze as she admired herself from all angles.

"It's perfect," Kiko whispered, in shock that the dress fit Joey's style to a T.

"It really is," Nicole agreed.

Chelle just nodded, too choked up to speak. She and Joey made eye contact in the mirror and exchanged a heartfelt look of genuine love. Despite all the jokes, they were the closest out of the crew. Their souls sensed a kindred spirit in heartbreak and love. They instinctively knew how to balance the other out and be supportive without enabling.

"Everything else is a piece of cake after this," Kiko exclaimed.

"Oh my God," Joey cried out. "We need a cake! Where are we going to get a good cake from on such short notice?"

"Joey is the only person I know who would postpone marrying the love of her life over a cake," Nicole teased.

"I have an idea," Chelle called out. "Do you think Dom's mother can make a cake? The one she made for your wedding was out of this world."

"Uh huh," Kiko nodded. "She can bake the rum cake and bring our foodie princess one of her favorite vanilla sheet cakes."

"I'm a simple gal," Joey drawled. "And I approve of all of this."

"Well, then we have to fly our mothers down because mine will run off with our children if she finds out she wasn't here for this," Nicole warned.

"I guess these are the benefits of dating athletes," Chelle mused. "Remy might have to try out for the NBA so we can spend money like this, too!"

"Girl, hush. I know you and Remy are ballin' on the low with that roster of clients you have," Kiko replied.

Chelle just shrugged, but her smile proved that Kiko was close, if not right.

"So, when we say mothers, that includes yours too," Nicole said to Joey, who sighed at the thought. She and her mother were in a neutral place, speaking occasionally, and Joey visited her a few times a year, but they weren't close. Had never been close.

"This is getting complicated because Shane's mother is in Europe somewhere, and she didn't fly back for his father's funeral, which hurt him. I doubt she'd fly in last minute for a wedding."

"Damn," Chelle muttered. "That's cold-blooded. I know his parents were separated, but to not attend to his funeral?"

"I think I'm understanding things a bit better," Nicole said. "I'm glad you and Shane did find each other. You needed each other."

Joey flashed a small smile and nodded, remembering what it was like when she felt all alone, but Shane was like a light shining through the darkness. "Yeah, we did."

"Ok, so invite your mothers to the reception," Kiko confirmed.

"And, technically, you're closer to all of our mothers anyway. I know mine loves you to death," Nicole stated.

"That's true. But what about Remy and Chelle's parents? Are we flying them in from New York?"

"Wait. Wait. Wait," Joey said, putting up her hands. "This is too much for a cake, even for me!"

"How about one of us just goes and gets the damn cake. Miami is an hour away. All our parents can be mad as hell that we didn't invite them. But if we invite one, we gotta invite all," Kiko said.

"Nope. We can bake a damn vanilla cake with frosting. Y'all are doing too damn much," Chelle said, shutting them all down. "You can have a cake from every state at your reception."

"You can even import a fruit tart from Italy," Nicole said slyly.

Kiko squinted at Joey. "I knew you and Shane were up to no good. Y'all were banging in Italy. Weren't you?"

"Girl, yes," Nicole replied. "These nasty mofos hooked up on the damn yacht when I was dying of seasickness."

"Nicole!" Joey just glared at her like she was betrayed.

"Jay busted you guys. He said he has a highlight reel in his mind of all the times he's caught you and Shane in the act."

"Guys, please," Kiko clapped her hands. "Focus. So, the cake is decided. Let's get this dress altered and get out of here. We still have shit to plan, and I want to enjoy some of my time off."

"Yes, ma'am!" Joey saluted her like a soldier in the military.

Chapter 16

The following two days passed at hyperspeed. Between getting permission to use the property as a site for the wedding and arranging for the beach to be transformed to hold the ceremony, Kiko and the girls knocked off task after task. After talking with Shane, Joey decided to extend the invitation to all their parents. Those who could come would be flown in, and those who couldn't make it would just attend the reception.

Everyone loved the idea of the spontaneous wedding and worked with Joey to get her what she needed for the big day. The dressmaker tailored the dress for her the same day she purchased it. The chef who catered their breakfast agreed to provide the dinner for the wedding and suggested someone to do the hors d'oeuvres. Of course, there were concessions for other guests, like Shane's friend, Damien, and Mallory, who offered to procure the cake and fly down with Nicole's mother and the babies.

They transformed one of the extra rooms into the bridal suite and the other into the groom's room. The morning of the wedding, Joey and Shane parted ways, with her making him promise that he wouldn't ruin things by trying to see her before the time. Shane wasn't very superstitious and said he couldn't agree to that, so Mallory was put on duty to ensure he didn't try anything. She was guiding the hairdresser to the suite when Shane pretended to be stalking in the hallway. Mallory shoved him back down the hallway toward the guys.

"Please keep your friend from trying to see his soon-to-be wife before it's time!" She pointed a finger at Damien, who looked around, perplexed.

"Me?" He pointed to himself.

"Yes. You." She pointed at him again. "If I have to make sure he doesn't crash the bridal suite, you have to be in charge of him."

They remained in a standoff for a moment, and Mallory felt a twinge of heat running up her spine as Damien gave her a long once-over. She thought him checking her out at the airport was a figment of her imagination, but now she had no doubt. Trying her hardest not to blush, she squinted her eyes and reiterated her point.

"So, you will keep an eye on him, right?" She raised her brows in question, ignoring how his eyes crinkled when he smiled.

"Got it, Chief," he replied with a salute.

"Good," she nodded before turning away. Unable to resist looking back over her shoulder, she found him watching her walk away with a mischievous smirk twisting his lips.

Inside the bridal suite, Joey was being prepped and primped. Mallory had also brought a blonde lace-front wig for the occasion. Joey refused to deal with her natural hair and the humidity of the tropics. The hairstylist placed large barrel curls throughout the wig while Chelle painted Joey's toes a pastel yellow to coordinate with the bouquet and her engagement ring. Kiko did her makeup, keeping it light and playing up on Joey's soft features.

"Oh, you're such a pretty bride," Chelle said with a lump in her throat as she admired her friend.

"Stop. Don't you make me cry," Joey growled. She'd been trying to hold on to her giddiness.

"Chelle! Please go somewhere with that crying. If you make Joey ruin her makeup before she even gets down the aisle, it's me and you!"

"Yeah," Nicole agreed. "I'm holding it in. Keep it together!"

"Fine. I'll shut up," Chelle sniffed.

The girls were all quiet after that. Their emotions were running too high to carry on idle chit-chat. They'd already spent the entire night before talking about how happy they were for Joey. All the years of rumors and sneaking around culminating in a happy ending was like a fairytale.

"It's time," Mallory whispered, peeking in the door. "And the groom is getting restless."

"Let's go girls. Even though I'm seeing you now, I can't wait to see you walk down the aisle." Kiko blew her a kiss, and Nicole winked at her as they went to join the other guests. Joey and Shane chose not to have a wedding party due to the last-minute status. Still, Chelle would serve as the unofficial flower girl, and Mallory would help carry her train until she reached the carpeted path that led to Shane.

Chelle grabbed Joey's hand, silently walking to the patio door that led out to the backyard.

"You ready, Shawty?" Chelle mimicked Shane as she secured the veil to Joey's half-updo.

"See, you're on that bullshit," Joey pointed at Chelle but laughed in spite of the endearment. "I love you to death, but please hurry and spread those petals before I fall apart."

Joey was fanning her eyes, trying to keep the tears at bay. Chelle was already crying but gave her a quick nod in understanding and a kiss on the cheek before she stepped out the door.

Joey took a deep breath, one hand pressed to her stomach to calm herself. Standing there, she felt a sense of peace that settled her soul. She wasn't scared, nervous, or worried she was making a mistake. Her heart was full and bursting, and she was excited about the promise of the future with the man who understood her to the core. She smiled at herself in the mirror, tears of joy rimming her lids.

Mallory smiled at Joey and gave her arm a quick squeeze as she got behind her to attend to her long train. "Share My Life" by Kem ended, and when "The Promise" by Tracy Chapman began, Joey took the first official step to the rest of her life. Shane and Chelle picked the songs for the wedding, and as she looked out over the small crowd, the lyrics took her by surprise. She'd never heard the song before, but it was perfect.

When she turned the curve that put her and Shane in direct view of each other, her breath hitched as a range of expressions racked his face. His nervous smile turned to awe, then to a bigger smile at seeing her in her dress. He stood with his back straight, legs slightly spread, and hands clasped in front of him, his smile cracking as she closed the distance between them. Overcome with emotions, he dropped his head, pressing his chin into his chest in an attempt to hide his tears.

The last few steps until she reached him seemed like the longest of Joey's life. When he looked up again, red-rimmed eyes and wet lashes accompanied his smile, and her heart felt like it had to grow ten times its size to accommodate all the love she felt for him at that

moment. There was a collective murmur of
"aww" when the couple came face to face. Joey
wiped his tears away, and Shane held her hand
and kissed the center of her palm. Then they
turned to face Tori, who was dabbing at her own
tears and shaking her head.

"You two," she whispered while putting
away her towelette and pulling out her written
notes.

"We are gathered here today to celebrate
with Shane and Jonelle as they proclaim their
love and commitment to the world. We are
gathered to rejoice, with and for them, in the
new life they now undertake together."

She nodded toward Joey to recite her
vows.

"Shane, I vow to honor you, love you, and
cherish you as my husband today and every
day. I promise to be your navigator, best friend,
and wife. I promise to honor, love, and cherish
you through all life's adventures. Wherever we
go, we'll go together.

Shane nodded his head with a tearful
smile. He took a deep, steadying breath before
he stated his vow to her.

"Jonelle, my love," he began, causing her
tears to return. He cleared his throat before he
continued. "I promise to be your partner in all

things. Not possessing you but working with you as a part of a beautiful whole. I promise you my love and my trust. For one lifetime with you could never be enough. This is my eternal vow to you, my equal in all things."

"This man is a whole poet out here," Jay murmured to Nicole, causing Chelle to lean over and slap his hand when the friends all chuckled. Tori just shook her head and smiled before returning her attention to the couple.

"Shane and Jonelle have chosen rings to exchange with each other as a symbol of their unending love. The ring is an icon of your love and commitment to each other. Its circular shape represents the idea that you are always connected to each other and that your love is constant and unending."

Tori faced Joey and smiled warmly. "As you place this ring on Shane's finger, please repeat after me. With this ring, I thee wed and pledge you my love now and forever."

Joey sniffed before she repeated, "With this ring, I thee wed and pledge you my love now and forever." She trembled with emotion as she slipped the ring on Shane's long finger, making a silly face to the crowd as he wiggled them around. Everyone chuckled, and then Tori playfully cleared her throat and directed her attention to Shane.

"Shane, as you place this ring on Jonelle's finger, please repeat after me. With this ring, I thee wed and pledge you my love now and forever."

"With this ring, I thee wed and pledge you my love now and forever." He gently slid the ring on Joey's finger and gathered her hands in his as he looked intently into her eyes. Joey returned the same intensity as it seemed like their entire relationship flashed before them. Through it all, the unwavering bond of friendship and what they learned to be love never faltered.

"Shane and Jonelle. The relationship you enter into today must be grounded in the strength of your love and the power of your faith in each other. To make your relationship succeed will take unending love.
It will take trust, knowing in your hearts that you truly want what is best for one another, and learning and growing together. It will take faith to go forward together without knowing what the future holds.
If you both come freely, and understand the responsibility and work involved to make your relationship thrive and are committed to not only each other but your family, please take each other by the hands and reply, 'We do.'"
"We do," they affirmed in unison.
"In the presence of your family and friends, you have spoken the words and performed the rites that unite your lives. It is my legal right as a minister and my greatest joy

and privilege to declare you husband and wife. You may now kiss the bride." Tori gestured for them to consummate their vows with a kiss as she stepped back.

Shane first kissed Joey's forehead before he leaned down and scooped her up into his arms. Joey let out a surprised laugh, grasping his face in her hands before leaning down to kiss him. Slowly, he let her body slide down the length of his as he wrapped her in a tight embrace. The couple kissed like it was their first kiss all over again.

"When a Man Loves a Woman" blared through the speakers as the crowd clapped, catcalled, and laughed at their dramatic display of affection. After years of hiding, the couple had no problem displaying their love for everyone to see.

"Ok. Save some for the honeymoon," Tori said as she patted Shane's back.

The couple finally broke apart, slightly flustered but feeling euphoric. Shane lifted Joey's hand over her head, presenting his wife to the world. Of course, their friends bombarded them with hugs, congratulations, and tears. Chelle couldn't stop crying, and Nicole had to keep dabbing the corners of her eyes.

"That was one of the most beautiful things I've ever seen," Nicole sniffed as she slid an arm around Chelle as they watched the couple greet and thank the few guests in attendance.

Of course, all of their parents were in attendance. Even Shane and Joey's mothers, which was a feat to accomplish, but Kiko insisted it be done. Mallory flew in with Nicole's mother and the babies, Damien cut his vacation short to make it, and Shane's mother had actually flown in from overseas. Joey's parents arrived separately and made no contact with each other, but she was just happy they were there. Her mother jumped at the opportunity to fly on a private jet and brought all of Joey's siblings along with her man, who was the father of the last three.

It was a whole mess, but she was there, and Joey was happy about it.

"The Rest Of Our Lives" by Jagged Edge drifted through the speakers when Chelle clapped to get everyone's attention.

"It's time for the couple's first dance!" She ushered Shane and Joey together and everyone else off the dancefloor. Shane held Joey's hands as he looked into her eyes as "Love" by Musiq Soulchild played. It was the song he picked, per Chelle's demands, and he felt the lyrics matched his heart and everything he wanted to say to Joey. He touched his forehead to hers when his emotions threatened to get the best of him. Joey tried to swipe his tears away covertly, but there was no point when she was crying just as hard. He just took her hands and wrapped her arms around him as they began to sway to the music.

Joey had chosen "By Your Side" by Sade, and when it played, Shane held her even tighter. They had gone through a lot in their young lives and had each other's backs through everything.

"I can't believe today is real," he murmured against her temple. "Each moment just feels more surreal than the last."

"I've felt like I was in a dream for the last few days," Joey admitted. "I didn't even know I could feel this happy."

"Every day has been a dream since I met you," he professed.

"Shane," Joey said with a soft sob.

"You brought light to my world. You brought me security. Always being there for me, no matter what. I never want to experience how life felt without you in it."

"I love you so much," she cried.

"And I love Lil Juicy. She's all mine now."

"You need help," Joey giggled.

"I need a night nurse," he said with a wink.

"And I willingly signed up for your nonsense," she teased.

"Me and all my nonsense are yours. Forever."

"You promise?"

"I promise."

The rest of the night was just as ethereal. After the emotional display, Joey and Shane let loose and celebrated hard. While it wasn't a massive party like the one they planned when they returned to California, they had the time of their lives. The vibes were high, everyone was in good spirits, and the couple's happiness was palpable.

They danced so much that eventually, Joey just took her shoes off. Shane sang every love song, rapped every hip-hop song like he wrote it, and kissed his new wife every chance he got. He danced with all the moms and all the kids. Joey's siblings adored him, not only because he was an NBA star but also because he was fun and spoiled them all. He treated Joey's family as if they were his since he met them years back.

Even though they didn't have a honeymoon planned, that night, Shane arranged for them to take a quick flight to Jamaica as a surprise. Joey almost lost her mind when she saw Chelle and Remy rolling out their suitcases, and Kiko explained that she was, in fact, going to a different island with her husband. She teared up again as she said her goodbyes and thanked everyone for helping her have the best day of her life.

"You're acting like you're moving to another planet," Shane teased her as they left.

Two hours later, they were landing on yet another luscious tropical Island. Joey had been to Jamaica before, and it was one of her favorite island experiences. Shane had reserved a private villa for a week so they could have downtime and adventures if they wanted.

Once they were checked in and settled, the exhaustion set in.

"I can't even take a number," Joey yawned as she stared out at the frothy waves lapping at their private beach.

"You're not tapping out on me, wifey?"

"I need a shower; that's all I know."

"I have an idea. Come on," Shane said as he led her through their patio doors toward the beach, grabbing a few large towels on the way out. Once they reached the shoreline, he began to strip. His eyes twinkled with mischief as he waited for Joey to catch on.

"You're about to get in the water? It's almost 3 a.m."

"The ocean doesn't have a curfew," he chuckled.

"What about sharks?"

Shane just glared at her. "I think you know me well enough to know–"

"You probably paid the sharks to swim somewhere else," she joked.

"Something like that. Now, let's get you out of this dress."

He pulled her closer, unzipped the back of her dress, and helped her slip it off. Once they were both naked, he grabbed her hand again as they walked into the calm, clear water.

"Oh my God! This feels so good."

Joey groaned with pleasure as the lukewarm water sloshed against her skin as she wadded in, waist deep. Shane walked up behind her and kissed her on the neck. Joey turned to face him, lifting up on her tiptoes to kiss his chest. He lifted her into his arms, and she wrapped her legs around him.

They didn't need to exchange words as their lips connected and their bodies strained. Joey's passionate moans had Shane hard as granite, and he wasted no time positioning the head of his dick to her slick heat that he could feel even underwater. He inched his length inside of her until they both sighed with the satisfaction of being joined together. Joey braced her hands on his shoulders as she rode him slow and steady, her pussy clenching around him wildly because she had been fantasizing about how they would consummate their union all day.

When he grabbed her hips and started to lift and slam her down on his dick, she screamed with pleasure. Shane bit down on her shoulder as he felt the familiar tingles spreading from his balls up his shaft like wildfire. Being inside Joey always felt like visiting another dimension, and when he exploded inside her, he definitely saw stars.

Shane knew sex on the beach was on Joey's bucket list, and now it was his job to make sure she crossed off every entry.

Epilogue

L.A. was playing Phoenix, and the arena was packed to witness Shane Duncan play his former team for the first time. Having home-court advantage, the crowd was pumped to witness one of the best players in the league play for them. Enough Phoenix jerseys and paraphernalia were scattered about to make the atmosphere a little unhinged.

Joey watched from the sidelines as Shane took the court and dominated the game for four quarters. He was laser-focused, scoring a new personal best record of sixty points for the game. Her younger sister, Toya, who had just turned eighteen, cheered next to her, yelling, "That's my brother!" every time Shane did something remarkable.

Toya was in her first year of college and was attending Charles R. Drew University of Medicine and Science. She wanted to be like Joey and attend an HBCU but wasn't ready to be too far from home. She also worked part-time at Joey's dance studio. Their relationship was beginning to blossom, and Shane encouraged it. Of course, family meant everything to him because he didn't have any siblings growing up and wasn't very close with his parents.

Shane's team won by twenty points. The fans were in a frenzy, and the arena was still packed long after the game was over. Joey was talking to the dancers, who she also consulted with and taught choreography. She was finding her footing focusing on her passion instead of her old dream of being the Queen of Corporate America.

While she was congratulating the girls on a great half-time show, a ball bounced on the back of her leg. She bent down to pick it up, and when she turned around, Shane was grinning at her with that goofy look in his that reminded her why he was her favorite person in the whole world.

"You ready to go home, wifey?"

"You haven't gotten tired of saying that yet, huh?"

"Nope. And I never will."

He slung one arm around her and the other around Toya as he led his family out of the building. Joey smiled because she was living her dream. She'd gotten more than she ever imagined and was married to her best friend.

The end!

Will there be another story from the friends group. Yes, maybe more than one. Can you guess who they will be about?

One Last Thing...

If you enjoyed this book, I'd be very grateful if you'd post a short review on Amazon. Your support really does make a difference and I read all the reviews personally so I can get your feedback and make the next book even better.

About The Author

Olivia Linden is a best-selling author of steamy romance and romantic suspense stories with diverse characters. Her stories mix her big personality with a sexy yet humorous tone, weaving tales of passion and suspense that you can feel, branding you with her unique vibe. Find more of her stories on Amazon.com

Made in the USA
Middletown, DE
11 September 2024

60731954R00184